Darcy's Honorable Proposal

D0775444

By Zoe Burton

Darcy's Honorable Proposal

Zoe Burton

Published by Sweet Escapes Press

© 2023 Zoe Burton

Early drafts of this story were written and posted on Patreon and fan fiction forums in early 2023.

ISBN: 978-1-953138-29-3

Acknowledgements

First, I thank Jesus Christ for giving me the words to write and loving me unconditionally. I love you!

Thank you, Rose and Leenie, for your encouragement.

Last but not least, thanks go to my Patreon Patrons, whose faithful support awes and humbles me.

Dedication

This book is dedicated to Bill Suter, whose thirst for blood knows no bounds.

Chapter 1

Nineteen-year-old Elizabeth Bennet stood along the side of the elegant ballroom at Westerville Place, the home of a viscount known to her father's sister and brother-in-law, Mr. and Mrs. James Blackwell, making conversation with Lady Penelope Mays, her host's sister. She did her best not to squirm, but she was eager to be on the move again. She had thus far avoided a certain baron but knew that the longer she remained in one place, the more likely it was that he would locate her in the crowded room.

Lady Penelope was everything Elizabeth did not wish to be, but she politely soldiered through the conversation, determined to remain civil despite the clear disdain the lady increasingly revealed.

"What did you say the name of your estate was?" Lady Penelope looked down her lifted nose.

Elizabeth summoned the best smile she could manage and pasted it to her face. "Longbourn, my lady. I doubt you have heard of it. It is significant in the county, but not what one would call a great estate."

"Indeed." Lady Penelope sniffed. "And its location? Herefordshire?"

Unclenching her jaw enough to reply, Elizabeth offered up the name but nothing else. "Hertfordshire."

"Oh, yes." Lady Penelope looked her up and down. "I am unfamiliar with your family, but I suppose that should not be a shock. One cannot know everyone, can one?"

"Not at all." Elizabeth noted with no small amount of relief that another lady was approaching her and her companion. She took advantage of the situation to remove herself from the tiresome conversation.

"Could you perhaps direct me to the retiring room? I need to refresh myself, and I am afraid that dancing and conversation have crowded its location out of my memory." She gripped her hands together tightly as she waited for Lady Penelope to turn her attention from whatever had drawn it.

The lady's eyes suddenly flicked toward Elizabeth. "The retiring room?" She glanced again to where she had been looking before and then turned back. Her gaze narrowed and a smirk lifted one corner of her lips. "Why, it is just across the hall from the doors." She pointed to a doorway a few feet away. "You cannot miss it."

Elizabeth followed Lady Penelope's pointing finger and, locating the pair of wood panels the woman indicated, looked at her companion once more. "Thank you, my lady." She curtseyed. "Perhaps we may finish our conversation another time."

The other woman's attention was now captured by the newcomer to arrive at her side, so she simply waved her hand in acknowledgment.

Elizabeth turned and hastened toward the indicated doors. She had not lied ... she did need to refresh herself ... but she also needed a moment alone. Arriving at the opening in the wall, she saw the door across the corridor, just where Lady Penelope had said it was. She paused to look over her shoulder and make a quick scan of the people nearby, then strode into the passageway. As she did, the musicians stopped playing, she supposed to take a break, as that was something they usually did at about this time at a ball. She pushed open the door and stepped inside.

Elizabeth's brow creased as she looked around the room. This did not look like a typical ladies' retiring room. There were the usual screens, but no maids and no mirrors or dressing tables. She stood just inside the door and turned to her left. She had not pushed the wooden panel shut just yet. She bit her lip, undecided about what to do. Should she leave the room and check with a servant that she was in the correct place? Or should she go behind a screen and use the chamber pot that was certain to be there before going back to the ballroom?

"Pardon me, madam. Are you looking for someone?"

The deep, disapproving voice startled her

and made her jump, a scream tearing out of her throat. She spun around to see who was behind her, but as she did so, her foot caught in her hem. She stumbled and fell forward, arms instinctively reaching out for something to grab onto.

The gentleman who had surprised her reacted quickly, grabbing her upper arms. However, he was unable to stop her fall. He staggered backwards as she fell into him, and the sleeves of her gown ripped off into his hands when she bounced off and landed on the floor at his feet.

Elizabeth immediately sat up, wincing at the twinges of pain in her knees and side. She stilled as she realized that her gown was ripped.

"Oh, no," she whispered, gathering the front of her bodice up to cover her once more. She started to look up when another voice drew her attention to the door.

"Why, Mr. Darcy and Miss Bennet, whatever are you doing in here?"

Elizabeth looked up to find Lady Penelope in the doorway. Beside and around her were other ladies and gentlemen. She opened her mouth to explain but before she could, someone else spoke.

"An assignation!"

Gasps arose behind the increasingly large crowd.

Lady Penelope, a smile on her face that

could only be described as smug, spoke again. "Look, she is practically undressed. I daresay we interrupted before they could get very far. I suppose we should not expect better of either of them. He clearly enticed her and she, stupid chit that she is, did not have the wits enough to say no." Her derision caused the crowd to laugh.

A growing feeling of terror grew in the region of Elizabeth's heart. She swallowed, determined not to give in to the feeling, and soon felt her courage rise, as it always did when someone attempted to intimidate her. "It is not what it apparently appears. This gentleman startled me and I tripped on my hem."

A lady Elizabeth did not know started to speak. "I can see how that could have happened. Mr. Darcy is lucky she did not-" The young woman fell silent when Lady Penelope turned to stare at her. She lowered her head and retreated.

Lady Penelope turned back toward the pair in the room and chuckled. Her derision was clear to her target when she replied. "That is what they all say. *I* say Mr. Darcy is a rake and a rogue and you have been revealed as nothing but a lackwitted trollop who fell for his lies."

Elizabeth's mouth opened to defend herself when the gentleman beside her stopped her.

"It will do no good to say anything else, madam. I see what is at play here."

9

Elizabeth looked up at him, her brow creasing. She pressed her lips together, unhappy to be in the position she was in, both literally and figuratively. She watched as he continued to speak, handing her sleeves back to her and shrugging out of his tailcoat.

"Here, take my coat and put it on. It will cover your gown. Who may we call for you?" He squatted down between Elizabeth and the crowd, swirling his coat behind her so it settled on her shoulders and holding it as she slid her arms into the sleeves.

She did not have time to tell him who she was with, for at just that moment, her aunt pushed past the crowd and entered the room.

"Elizabeth? What has happened?"

"Oh, Aunt." Her courage suddenly crumbling, tears filled her eyes. She could barely see the gentleman in front of her stand and hold out his hand. She placed her palm in his and allowed him to help her up, and the moment she was on her feet, she stepped into her Aunt Blackwell's loving embrace.

~~~***~~~

Fitzwilliam Darcy watched as the pretty young lady who had wandered into the gentlemen's retiring room sobbed in the arms of the older lady she called aunt. He surreptitiously shook out his hand, which still tingled from the touch of her palm when he helped her to rise from her position on the floor. His attention was drawn away when an older gentleman entered on the heels of Viscount Westerville. His friend said nothing, merely cocking an eyebrow before turning to the crowd and shooing them away.

"There is nothing to see here. Go on back to the ball. You, too, Penelope." He made a motion with his hands. "Off with you now. Go find Mama and sit with her."

Darcy ignored the grin of triumph Lady Penelope threw his way as she turned to obey her brother's directive. Instead, he turned back toward the young lady and her aunt, who had been joined by a gentleman he recognized from his club, Mr. James Blackwell.

"What has happened here?" Blackwell turned toward Darcy. "Mr. Darcy." He bowed. "I am even more shocked that you are involved than I am that my niece is. Do you have an explanation?"

Darcy returned Blackwell's bow. "I do; it is an unfortunate accident – two of them, actually – that has led to the current situation. I do not have proof and we will have to apply to the young lady for confirmation, but I believe another guest directed her into this room for reasons that I can guess at but again have no proof of. Your niece was facing away from me when I came up behind her and spoke. She was startled and when she turned toward me, she stumbled, with the results that you can see."

Blackwell's brow creased. "Who would do such a thing?"

Darcy hesitated. Before he could speak, the girl, whose sobs had quieted somewhat, did.

"Lady Penelope told me this was the retiring room. I had forgotten its location, so I inquired of her, since we were already in conversation." Elizabeth sobbed once but lifted her hand to cover her face and appeared to swallow the next one. "I was about to leave the room and find a servant to ask when this gentleman frightened me."

Viscount Westerville moved closer. "My sister directed you here?"

Elizabeth nodded. "She did. I do not know why, because this clearly is not the *ladies'* retiring room. Should she not have understood that is where I wished to go?"

The viscount shook his head. "One would think she would, but my sister can be a vindictive chit, and Darcy recently made it clear to her that he was uninterested in making her the mistress of Pemberley." He turned to his friend. "Did you not?"

Darcy rolled his eyes. "I did. I never imagined she would retaliate, much less do such a thing as this." He waved his hand toward Elizabeth.

A knock on the door startled the group, and Westerville called out for the party to enter. "Come."

The door opened and another girl, this one with blonde hair and big blue eyes timidly entered, trailed by another of Darcy's friends, Mr. Charles Bingley. "I am sorry. I was looking for -." She paused, her hand going to her mouth when she saw Elizabeth. Rushing forward, she opened her arms. "Oh, Lizzy. Are you well?"

Elizabeth nodded, letting go of her aunt to receive her sister's hug. "I am; or at least, I will be."

Mrs. Blackwell looked at her oldest niece with concern in her eyes. "How did you know to come here, Jane? You and Mr. Bingley were drinking punch when I left you."

Jane blushed, looking suddenly uneasy. "I noticed many other guests whispering amongst themselves and happened to overhear Lizzy's name and location. I thought I should find her and see if she needed assistance." She hugged her sister close again. "It is not like her to do anything to cause that sort of attention to be drawn to her and I was concerned."

Darcy glanced at Bingley, who had stepped up beside him. "Is this true?"

Bingley nodded, turning his gaze from the sisters to Darcy. "Unfortunately, it is. We could not hear everything that was said, but based on the reactions of those around us, I knew it was bad." He paused. "Your name was also being bandied about, which is why I fol-

13

lowed. What Miss Bennet has said of her sister is also true of you. You are not one to do anything that might cross the lines of propriety. I was concerned about you."

"Thank you, Bingley. You have always been an excellent friend." Darcy squeezed Bingley's shoulder.

Chapter 2

"Well." The viscount startled Darcy when he suddenly spoke. "It seems we have a bit of a conundrum on our hands here."

Mr. Blackwell instantly agreed. "Yes, we do." He turned to Darcy. "Forgive me, but we will need to have a discussion and I am uncertain you have ever met my family."

Darcy tilted his head. "I have not. Will you introduce them?"

"Certainly." Blackwell gestured toward the three ladies. "Please meet my wife, Annabelle, and my nieces, Miss Jane Bennet and Miss Elizabeth Bennet of Longbourn in Hertfordshire. Ladies ..." He motioned toward Darcy. "Please meet Mr. Fitzwilliam Darcy of London and Pemberley in Derbyshire. Beside him is Mr. Charles Bingley, and behind him, of course, is our host, the Viscount Westerville."

"I am pleased to make your acquaintance." Darcy bowed.

"I think it would be a good idea to move our discussion somewhere else. I offer you the use of my study." Westerville waved his hand in the direction of the door. "I have already shooed away three gentlemen. I am certain no one wishes for what is to transpire to be overheard."

Darcy dipped his chin and looked toward Elizabeth and her family.

"Indeed." Blackwell nodded and turned to his wife and nieces. "Mrs. Blackwell, why do you not take Jane back to the ballroom? It is best if we pretend nothing is amiss." He next spoke to Jane. "You must take care, my dear. People of high society are often unpleasant, and what has happened with your sister may well cause some to say things to you that are inappropriate. If you hear anything untoward, especially from a gentleman, you are to immediately return to your aunt's side. You are far too apt to see the best in everyone." He took Jane's hand in his and patted the back. "Do you understand what I am saying to you? Look for hidden meanings and agendas."

"Yes, sir; I will." Jane gave Blackwell a gentle smile and turned toward her sister. "You will have Uncle send for me if you need me, will you not?"

"I will." Elizabeth hugged Jane. "Thank you," she whispered.

Jane smiled again and turned. She tucked her hand into the crook of the elbow Bingley offered her and allowed him to escort her out the door.

Darcy followed the rest of the group into the hallway as Westerville led them to the staircase and up one floor. He felt as though he were watching himself from outside of his body. It was almost as if he were someone else. He swallowed as he looked at the back of Miss Elizabeth Bennet's head. He knew in the recesses of his mind that he must do the honorable thing by her, which meant a proposal of marriage. However, he did not know her. For all he knew, she was as empty-headed as most of the debutantes he had been introduced to the last few seasons. Worse, she could be manipulative and vindictive, like Lady Penelope. He looked down, seeing the pattern in the carpet pass under his feet as he walked. He took a deep breath and then exhaled, puffing his cheeks out as he did so. As he followed the group into Westerville's study, he squared his shoulders and lifted his chin. He was a Darcy, and he took his family name and reputation seriously. He would do what was expected.

~~~***~~~

Elizabeth followed her uncle and the viscount into the dimly lit room and waited for Westerville to light some additional candles. Her bout of tears had led to a massive, pounding headache, and all she wished to do was go home and curl up in bed. *I just want this all to be over with,* she thought. She was uneasy. She knew what would likely transpire in the discussion that was about to happen, and she did not want to deal with it. She had always longed to marry for love. She wished to esteem and respect her husband. She had no desire to wed someone she did not know. *Surely, no one will force me to marry this man!* She thought of her father, at home at Longbourn. He would laugh at her situation, but she was certain he would not force her into a marriage she did not want. She bit her lip. Mr. Darcy was a stranger, a man she was not acquainted with. She did not want a marriage like her parents had and that is exactly what she would get if she did not speak up for herself and refuse to accept him. She straightened her shoulders under his coat and lifted her chin.

When he had the room lit up, Westerville gestured to a seating area in front of the fire-place. "Make yourselves comfortable." He strode to the bell pull and rang for a servant.

Elizabeth and her uncle sat on a sofa together. She watched Darcy sit on a wingback chair close to the fire. She opened her mouth to speak, but her uncle beat her to it.

"There is only one solution to this dilemma. Surely you must see that, Mr. Darcy."

Darcy's mouth drew down at the corners. To Elizabeth, he looked to be exceedingly displeased. "Unfortunately, I do."

At that moment, Westerville admitted a servant to stoke up the fire, and all conversation ceased until the maid was finished with her work and was dismissed. Elizabeth watched as their host joined them, settling into a chair that matched Darcy's but was on the other side of the fire, nearer to Elizabeth's end of the sofa.

"Well, then. Where were we?" Westerville sat up straight. "Where are my manners? Can

I pour anyone a drink?"

Though Elizabeth declined, wanting nothing more than to get said whatever needed to be, the gentlemen all decided they wished for port, so the viscount hopped up again and poured them all drinks. Elizabeth rolled her eyes but said nothing.

Blackwell accepted the glass of port handed to him. "Mr. Darcy and I were just saying that there is but one honorable resolution to the events of this evening."

"Indeed." The viscount settled down into his chair again. He eyed Elizabeth and then her uncle before turning to Darcy. "I am sorry, old man. I am certain you agree, though. The young lady did not try to trap you, if what she says is true, and we both know Penelope is perfectly capable of doing such a thing. Even if we could get her to admit it and publicly apologize, there are those who would still consider Blackwell's niece to be ruined. She would be an outcast, as would all her family."

Darcy nodded, his expression somber. "I am aware of all of that." He sighed, frowning into his glass. "I do not like being forced." He lifted his head when Elizabeth spoke.

"Neither do I!" She turned to her uncle. "There must be another solution. There has to be!" She waved her hand around. "Surely by this time tomorrow there will be some other scandal to catch society's attention, and then all will be as it was. There is no need for such a spectacular step as marriage to be taken!"

Darcy's attention was arrested by Elizabeth's vehemence. Clearly, she did not care about his fortune. He assumed she knew of it; did not every single female in London? Why was she so insistent that she would not wed him?

"I am afraid that if Lady Penelope has spread word of the event, our names will be linked in every drawing room in Mayfair by noon tomorrow. As much as I would like to agree with you, Miss Bennet, and see us each go our separate ways, it will not be possible." Darcy leaned forward, placed his glass on the table beside him, and clasped his hands between his knees as he addressed her. "As my friend Bingley indicated, I have never done anything to besmirch my family's name. I have no intentions of beginning now. I have always behaved honorably, and I can promise to treat you with respect."

"Think of your sister, Lizzy." Blackwell turned on the sofa to face his niece. "Jane should not have to suffer because people think less of you." He held up his hand. "I am undoubtedly saying this badly, and I expect your aunt to demand a full accounting of my words and then give me a proper dressing-down. I know you have not behaved improperly. You entered that room at the instigation of another and had every intention of exiting it. Mr. Darcy is also above reproach. He is doing the right thing, or trying to. But, only the four of us in this room are aware of it." He pointed to each of the gentlemen and to Elizabeth. "It is not we who will be gossiping and making judgements. It will be the ladies and gentlemen in that ballroom, and it will be those same people who may cut your sister for what they perceive as your poor behavior."

"I do not wish to end up in a marriage like the one I see every day at Longbourn." Elizabeth spoke heatedly, glancing as she did so toward the viscount and Darcy. Turning back to her uncle, she continued to argue. "I do not want Jane to suffer, but I am nothing to these people and I refuse to believe they will be speaking of me in any manner at all once the ball is over and they have returned to their homes."

"May I make a suggestion, as a disinterested observer?" The viscount looked at each of them as he spoke, waiting until each had nodded their unspoken permission before he continued. "Emotions are high at the moment. I suggest Blackwell take Miss Bennet home for the night and allow her to sleep on it. Miss Bennet, take the time to consider my friend. He really is a good man and taking his name will be advantageous in many ways. Darcy can visit tomorrow and things can be discussed with clearer heads. Maybe he will even actually propose instead of just dancing around the topic." Westerville smirked. "What do you say?"

Blackwell looked at Darcy. "I think that is a

very sensible idea. My home will be open to you, sir, as soon as you arrive, no matter the time."

Darcy nodded slowly, taking a deep breath. "I agree, as well. Thank you, Westerville, for thinking of it. We are doing ourselves no good here. I believe I will also go home. I am in no mood to defend myself from the allegations I am sure are going around out there." He stood and the rest followed. "I will visit you tomorrow, Miss Bennet, but I will check the scandal sheets first to see if any mention of the event has made it to the papers. If by some miracle it has not, you may have your way." He bowed. "Good night, madam." He bowed to the other gentlemen, accepted the goodbyes and bows of the rest, and waited while Blackwell escorted his niece out of the room and down the back stairs. With a sigh, he followed his friend to the front door, accepting his coat, hat, and gloves from a footman.

"Thank you for your support."

Westerville clasped his hand over Darcy's shoulder. "Always. I am sorry this has happened." He glanced in the direction of the ballroom. "I do not know what to say about Penelope. Mother has always spoiled her and it has grown worse since Father's passing. I will do what I can to censure her, though I am certain I will be overruled. However, she cannot go around seeking revenge on everyone who angers her, and I will stress that to her the best I can." He smirked. "I may need to borrow a room at your house for a few days, though."

Darcy shook his head and looked down, hiding a roll of his eyes. He brought his gaze back up to his friend's, his lips twisting. "You are always welcome, as you very well know. You are, however, a viscount. Surely that gives you more power over your household than the average man would have."

Westerville's laugh boomed around the entry. "Sadly, the women in my life are not afraid of my title." He laughed again. "Good night, my friend."

"Good night." Darcy bowed once more and then turned, placing his hat on his head and walking out into the cold, dark night. He settled into his waiting carriage, his mind on the events of the evening. He tapped his cane on the roof and looked out the window as the equipage lurched into motion.

A few minutes later, he was alighting from his carriage in front of Darcy House, never so glad to be home.

Chapter 3

It was early the next afternoon when Darcy knocked on the Blackwells' door. He was directed to a drawing room, where he found a red-eyed Miss Elizabeth Bennet, her worried-looking sister and aunt, and her grim-faced uncle. He bowed to each.

Producing a folded newssheet and gesturing towards them, he inquired if they'd read it. "I assume that you have all read the papers this morning."

"Come in and sit, Mr. Darcy." Blackwell nodded toward the seating area where his family was located. "We have, indeed, been accosted by the news and in a tragically shocking manner."

Startled, Darcy felt his brows rise as he lowered himself into a chair. "What do you mean?"

"My wife and eldest niece visited the modiste this morning, where they were treated abominably by nearly everyone they came into contact with. Tell him, my dear."

Mrs. Blackwell lifted her chin. "The seamstresses at the modiste's establishment were rude, but that was not the worst of it. A group of young ladies came up to us and spoke to us directly about what happened last night, insinuating that you and Lizzy had been caught in the act of behaving as a married couple.

Others were nearby when we stopped for tea and were ..." She lifted her hands and made a motion with her forefingers. "'Whispering' about it loudly enough that everyone in the tables near them could hear that the Bennet girls were trollops who did unspeakable things with gentlemen." Her jaw worked and she swallowed. "They wondered about Blackwell and myself, speculating that we were ..." She swallowed again, breathing deeply through her nose. "They speculated that we were prostituting our nieces out and called us procurers." Her lips quivered as she finished and she pressed them together into a tight line.

Darcy was stunned. This was far worse than what he had read in the papers.

"I do not know what to say." He leaned forward. "I am truly sorry this has happened." He shook his head. "Would that I had not frightened you last night, Miss Elizabeth. If I had approached you differently, or simply waited to see what you would do before speaking, none of this would have happened. I apologize for my part in this fiasco."

Elizabeth, who had begun crying as her aunt spoke, wiped her eyes. "Thank you, sir," she whispered. "If I had asked anyone else to direct me, or had immediately turned and left the room the second I realized it looked off, this would not have happened. I do not think blame can be cast on anyone here. That lies with someone else."

Darcy nodded. His jaw clenched as he considered the terrible price the ladies of this house had suffered because of the jealous vindictiveness of someone else. He took a deep breath.

"I think it is clear now what our path needs to be; do you not agree, Blackwell?" He looked at his host.

"I do." Blackwell turned to Elizabeth. "We spoke of this as a possibility last night. You have heard what happened to your aunt and sister. What think you now?"

Elizabeth opened her mouth to speak, but Darcy's voice stopped her. "I would like a private audience with Miss Elizabeth. It is possible that I have the means of assuring her of her future happiness."

Blackwell pressed his lips together and looked at his wife. Whatever he saw must have decided him, for he stood and said, "Very well. I will take Annabelle and Jane into another room. We will leave the door open a little, and I will stand out in the hall beside it." He looked at Elizabeth and opened his mouth as though to speak but ended up closing it and shaking his head. He turned and escorted the other ladies out of the room.

There was a long moment of silence between Darcy and Elizabeth once the others had gone. Finally, he cleared his throat. "I am so sorry for the distress you are experiencing." He sighed and looked at the papers in his hand. "I did not show these to your uncle. I assume he has already seen them." He extended them toward her. "Have you?"

Elizabeth shook her head. She mouthed the word "no," then cleared her throat. "No," she said clearly. "I have not." She hesitated but reached her hand out to accept the sheets. Darcy had folded them so that the society pages of each of the two papers were facing up. There, in black and white, were the words that proved that all of society thought her a walking scandal.

> *This reporter has it on good authority that the haughty and arrogant Mr. D. of Derbyshire has the same feet of clay as the rest of us. He was caught in flagrante, as they say, with Miss E. B. of Hertfordshire. It seems the rumors about country girls are correct and that milkmaids make the best lovers.*

Elizabeth gasped, her hand coming up to cover her mouth. She stood, staring at the words in her hands. "I did not ... we did not ... where did they come up with this?"

Darcy had risen to his feet when she did, and he now reached to take the newspapers from her and set them on the table next to his chair. He grasped her hands in his and looked earnestly into her eyes. "They did as they always do and took poetic license with a vague rumor. Though I am almost certain the *on dit* was passed on to the reporter by Lady Penelope, or, at least, at her bidding." He sighed and then continued in as gentle a manner as he could. "There is more." When she looked up at him, he gazed directly into her eyes. "I sent my valet out early this morning to do some snooping around. He is very good at ferreting out information. What he heard was that Lady Penelope was proud of herself for her actions. She crowed about it to her maid, who told the entire household staff, one of whom shared the story with Smith. I am certain that even in Hertfordshire, once the servants know, everyone knows." He watched as she closed her eyes and looked like she might cry. He found himself wishing to draw her close and comfort her, a feeling that surprised him and one he resisted. "Does this information help you make a decision?"

Elizabeth nodded. "Yes." She licked her lips. "It does."

"Very well." Darcy lowered himself to one knee. "Miss Bennet, I know that we are strangers who have been thrown into an impossible situation. You are barely acquainted with me and I with you. We could be completely incompatible for all we know. However, to save our reputations, it is imperative that we marry and do it soon. I promise you, as God is my witness, that if you agree to wed me, I will be faithful to you and show you respect. I will not dismiss your concerns as I see other men do to their wives, nor will I make decisions for you, though I do retain the right to have the final word on matters pertaining to the family as a whole. But, I promise to consult you in all things and to do my best to grow to love you and make you love me. Will you marry me?"

Elizabeth took a deep breath. "You have relieved a great fear of mine with your words. I would have insisted on respect whether you offered it freely or not. However, since you did offer it, and I have been made aware how low I have been forced to fall and how I have dragged my dearest sister down with me, I will accept your proposal. Yes, Mr. Darcy, I will marry you. Thank you."

Darcy closed his eyes in relief. He did not understand why he felt so strongly about her acceptance. After all, though they were currently being spoken of negatively, if he had decided to walk away, she would have been the only one of the two of them whose reputation would have suffered long-term damage. He did care, though. He had found over the course of the night that he did not mind the thought of being married to Elizabeth Bennet. He smiled as he rose to his feet.

"Thank you." He lifted her hands to his mouth and kissed her fingers. "You will not regret it."

Elizabeth's lips twitched upward into a brief, weak smile. "I hope not, sir."

A knock sounded on the door frame and Elizabeth's uncle's head popped into the opening. "How are things going in here?"

Darcy's deep voice gave its reply. "I have proposed, and Miss Bennet has accepted me."

Blackwell's eyes closed briefly as his head dropped. He seemed to take in a great, deep breath. Then, he straightened and entered the room. "Excellent! I would like to invite you to break your fast with us, sir. After that, we can discuss the settlement and write to Bennet with the news."

"Thank you; I accept the offer of breakfast." Darcy tilted his head for a moment. "I assume this Bennet you speak of is my betrothed's father?"

Blackwell gestured toward the hallway. "This way, if you please." He led the couple out of the room and up the stairs. "We are breaking our fast in the upstairs sitting room this morning. To answer your question, yes, Bennet is my brother-in-law. He has given me authority to act in his behalf if either of the girls found a suitor. I have a general idea of what their settlements should look like, and I will write to him express and ask him for any additional details we need."

They had arrived at the room where the ladies had gathered. Darcy asked, "Should I ride out to Hertfordshire and speak to him myself?" He was startled to see Elizabeth go pale.

"I can assure you there is no need." Black-

31

well waved the pair to seats at the table in the corner, near the window. "You certainly can if you wish, but it is unnecessary." He turned his attention to his wife and elder niece. "Ladies, I am happy to inform you that our Lizzy has accepted a proposal of marriage from Mr. Darcy. I was just telling him that he does not need to attend Mr. Bennet at Longbourn."

Darcy noticed Annabelle's eyes widen.

"Oh, no, you do not need to do that." She paused and bit her lip, then she sighed and her shoulders fell for a moment. "I am quite sure we sound odd, being so insistent on this. Let me just say that my brother's wife is quite … challenging … for one who is unfamiliar with her, and my brother seems to have followed in our father's path of indolence. Thomas does not take the time to check Fanny and, well …" She trailed off. "We just wish to spare you a bad head, I suppose."

"I see." Darcy had just pushed Elizabeth's chair in and was taking his own. He made use of the time to quickly contemplate what he had been told. The comparison to some of his own relations was uppermost in his mind. "I have a cousin on the Darcy side who is a trial to visit." Another thought struck him. "As a matter of fact, my maternal aunt, Lady Catherine de Bourgh is often difficult, as well, though perhaps for a different reason. We all have relatives we wished behaved differently, I wager. If you say that I have no need to visit Mr. Bennet, I am happy to remain in London." He paused again. "Would it be possible to invite him to town to review the settlement? Even if I were to approach the bishop, who is my uncle, to get a special license, it will be a few days before we can marry. Mr. Bennet might even be able to walk Elizabeth down the aisle."

Blackwell looked around the table, and Darcy noted that all the ladies nodded to him.

"That sounds like an excellent plan. I will invite him hither. He visits town but rarely, as he dislikes all the noise and dirt of the city, but I am certain he would come for this without question."

Chapter 4

Later that morning, once the family had broken their fasts and Blackwell had taken Darcy to his study to begin negotiating the marriage articles, Elizabeth, Jane, and Annabelle were seated in the drawing room. It was Annabelle's at-home day, and the ladies expected at least a few visitors, despite the scandal that was now attached to their names.

"At the very least, some will come to make sport of us," Annabelle said with a heavy sigh. "I have spoken to Somerset and instructed him to have footmen stationed inside the room, as well as just outside it. I wish your uncle could be here, but we shall have to make do without him."

Elizabeth closed her eyes to prevent another onslaught of tears. "I am sorry to have caused so much trouble," she said to her aunt.

Annabelle reached for her niece's right hand. "None of this is your fault, my dear, and I forbid you from taking credit for it." She squeezed the cold fingers. "Fault for this lies with Lady Penelope Mays and her band of followers. Not with you or with Mr. Darcy." She let go and sat back in her chair, her spine straight. "Now, hold your head up and look these harridans in the eye. You are a Bennet, a well-bred gentlewoman from an old family, a virtuous and capable lady."

Elizabeth gave her aunt a weak smile. "Thank you for your faith in me. I will do my best."

Jane, who sat beside her sister on the other side, took Elizabeth's left hand in hers. "Remember what you always say: your courage rises with every attempt to intimidate you."

Elizabeth snorted and then sighed. "It always has. I surely hope it does today, as well." She gripped her dearest sister's hand tightly.

The butler knocked and slipped into the room. He bowed to Annabelle.

"Yes, Somerset?"

The senior servant shifted on his feet as he glanced in Elizabeth's direction. "Madam, Sir Augustus Perry is demanding to be allowed in.

Elizabeth groaned. "Of all the rotten luck," she cried. "Why is *he* here?"

Mr. Somerset cleared his throat. "If it helps, he arrived at the same time as Mrs. Gardiner and a group of ladies, including Mrs. Rosenthorpe and Lady Ingledue."

"Yes, it does help." Annabelle turned to her nieces. "We must allow them all in. It would not do to create more of a stir by allowing the baron to make a scene when he was barred from the door."

Closing her eyes, Elizabeth silently cursed the situation. If she were in charge, she would not care about any fuss Sir Augustus made, but it was not her house and not her decision to make. She took a deep breath. "Very well, then."

Annabelle nodded and instructed Somerset

to bring the group in. She stood and Elizabeth and Jane followed suit.

The visitors were soon before them, and the ladies of the Blackwell household greeted them with the usual curtseys and welcomes. Elizabeth and Jane made room on the settee for their Aunt Gardiner to sit with them.

Though Elizabeth did her best to ignore the baron, she was acutely aware of his location in the room. She had caught a glimpse of his countenance when he realized her location and his lack of access to it, with her sister on one side of her and her aunt on the other. The expression on his face had caused a shiver to run up her spine.

The visit went as most do, with the exception of the stiltedness of the conversation. The women who made up this group were some of the biggest gossips in London and they were looking for all the juicy details they could get. Annabelle and her nieces, as well as Mrs. Gardiner, were tightlipped, however, and they had nothing to say, instead leaving their visitors to think whatever they wished. Thankfully, to Elizabeth's mind, their time was soon over and they were walking out the door.

Mrs. Gardiner remained standing after the wooden panel closed. "If you will excuse me," she said to her nieces and Annabelle, "I will be right back." She left the room just as the housekeeper entered to speak to the mistress.

Suddenly, Elizabeth found Sir Augustus at

her side. She pulled back in disgust.

"Miss Elizabeth, I am sorry to hear of your misfortune. I offer myself to you as a solution. Marry me, and your reputation will be restored."

Though she did not want this man to have any information about her whatsoever, she decided that telling him the truth was likely the fastest way to get rid of him. "Thank you for your kind offer, sir, but there is no need. I have already accepted an offer of marriage from Mr. Darcy."

"What?" Sir Augustus's eyes grew wide then narrowed. "Why would you accept him when you have me throwing myself at your feet?"

Elizabeth stared at him, her mouth falling open. "Sir, I have informed you before that we would not suit. If you recall, I declined your offer of a courtship just last week." Suddenly, her blood began to boil and she stood. "Why are you even here?" She barely heard Jane call her name and did not feel her sister's restraining hand on her arm.

The baron stood when she did. "I am here to offer consolation to you and to propose. You have a problem and I am the solution." He knelt on one knee and tried to take her hand. "Tell me you will make me the happiest of men and accept my proposal."

"No, I will not." Elizabeth felt herself go red. "I have long understood your character, sir, and I will not tie myself to someone whose negativity, arrogance, conceit, and selfish disdain for the feelings of others dominates his life. You could not have made application for my hand in any manner that would have induced me to accept you. I would rather live my life as an outcast from society, banished to a small island in the sea, than to marry you or anyone like you."

By this time, Elizabeth's voice had risen and Annabelle and Madeline had rushed back into the room and to her side, the butler and footmen following.

Annabelle inserted herself between her irate niece and the source of said niece's anger. "Sir, I must demand that you leave the premises immediately." She pointed to the door. "Go, now, or I will authorize my servants to force you to leave."

Sir Augustus appeared at this point to be every bit as angry as the object of his affection. "Very well," he snarled, "but this is not over. I will carry my point." He turned on his heel and stomped away.

Elizabeth watched him exit the room, closing her eyes and collapsing onto the settee when she saw the door shut behind him.

"Are you well, Lizzy?" Jane's voice was accompanied by a soothing hand that caressed her sister's brow.

"I am well." Though she wished to remain slumped in her seat, Elizabeth knew that to do so would distress all her family, so she took a deep breath and opened her eyes, sitting up straight.

Jane slid over on the settee a bit to give her room, and Madeline Gardiner resumed her place on Elizabeth's other side, rubbing her back.

"Are you certain about that?" Maddie tilted her head so she could take in the expression on her niece's face. "I am so sorry to have left you alone. I had to use the necessary and it never occurred to me that he was still in the room. I do not know what I was thinking."

Elizabeth shook her head. "Do not blame yourself." She squeezed her aunt's hand when the older woman took hers. "It would have happened eventually, no matter what precautions were taken." She sniffed back tears. "Thank you for coming. I did not intend to be the cause of disrupting your household, as well as this one."

Maddie smiled. "My household is as calm as ever. The children are quite well with their nanny and nursemaid. When your note came, I saw that you needed me more than they did and I was happy to attend you."

Annabelle had ordered a fresh pot of tea and now joined the rest of her family. "You are right, Lizzy; this event would have happened regardless. I have never seen a gentleman with as little awareness of the feelings of others as Sir Augustus Perry." She shook her head. "Still, I feel terribly that I also left an opening for him to accost you." A knock on the door interrupted her. "Come," she called.

The housekeeper bustled in trailed by a

maid carrying a silver tray. "Here is your fresh pot of tea, madam." She glanced at Elizabeth. "Is there anything else I can get for you? Something for Miss Elizabeth's nerves, perhaps?"

Despite her continued anger, Elizabeth chuckled. "Thank you, Mrs. West. I will be well once I have expressed my feelings and had quiet time to think."

The housekeeper smiled, her eyes softening. Elizabeth knew she was a favorite of the elder woman, and knew she would be pampered if she allowed it.

"I have had a pot of chocolate made for you, nonetheless. It can cure a variety of ills, you know. Especially when one adds the amount of sugar you do." Mrs. West winked, and the ladies all laughed.

"Thank you." Elizabeth looked the housekeeper in the eye. "Though I do not deserve or require it, it is very much appreciated."

Mrs. West blushed, but her eyes crinkled and her lips lifted again. She curtseyed and, when Annabelle excused her, exited the room, shooing the maid out before her.

Mrs. Blackwell settled herself into her chair and began to pour out Elizabeth's chocolate and fresh tea for the rest. "You are her favorite, you know. She would not go to such lengths unasked for anyone else, including me, and she was the very first servant I hired after I married nearly thirty years ago." She shook her head.

Elizabeth found it difficult to remain angry in the face of such affection. "I do know." She glanced at her sister. "She likes Jane, as well, though."

"But not as much as she likes you, Lizzy." Jane nudged her sister with her elbow. "You do not even have to ask for things. It is as if Mrs. West knows what you will request before you make one."

Elizabeth shook her head, a blush staining her cheeks. "I suppose you are correct, but I have never asked for or demanded special treatment."

"And that is why she favors you so." Maddie touched her younger niece's arm. "I would venture a guess that you remind her of someone from her past that she cared about." She smiled. "I suspect she likes the little bit of impertinence that you display every now and then. It can be quite refreshing, you know."

Annabelle laughed. "It can be. Mrs. West told me once that you remind her of her elder sister when they were young. They were very close. She lost that sibling to childbed twenty or thirty years ago, but her memories remain strong."

"How sad!" Jane pressed a hand to her chest. "I would be devastated to lose any of my sisters. Poor Mrs. West!"

"It is a fact of life, unfortunately." Annabelle sighed and looked at the clock. "We could receive more visitors at any time. Let us fortify ourselves just in case."

The ladies did just that. They were soon joined by Darcy and Blackwell. The group made small talk, with Darcy taking Maddy's place at Elizabeth's side.

"You and my uncle have worked out my settlement, then, sir?" Elizabeth tilted her head briefly to glance at her betrothed, then looked back down at her plate, which she had balanced on her lap, and her cup of chocolate. She involuntarily shivered when his deep voice washed over her.

"We have." Darcy sipped his tea. "A letter has been written to your father, inviting him to town to meet me and approve the final copy. I offered to post it, but your uncle handed it off to one of his servants."

Elizabeth nodded. "Probably to Somerset. He has a nephew who works in the stable and who is a jockey on his days off. My uncle keeps a retired racehorse and Jack is the one who exercises it. When there is an express to be sent off, that is who usually performs the office. Though the cost of keeping an extra horse is significant, an express will get to its destination faster for not having to wait for the postal service."

Darcy smiled. "I utilize one of my stable boys in a similar manner, though none of them are jockeys and I keep no race horses."

Elizabeth chuckled. "I know no one else who does." She glanced at him again. "I suspect my uncle has reasons for keeping the animal that he chooses not to share with anyone, though I have heard my aunt interrogate him once or twice."

Darcy grinned and looked at his plate. He took a bite of cheese and when he had swallowed it, spoke again. "I will go today to visit the archbishop. I foresee no issues with getting a special license. I have the funds, and my family is old enough and of sufficient status that no one should look askance at it even without the family connection."

Elizabeth nodded. She wondered why she did not feel more distress at his words than she did. "Good." She took a deep breath. "The more smoothly this process goes, the better I will feel."

"We are in agreement with this." He flashed her a quick smile. "I meant what I said earlier. I believe that husbands should be faithful to their wives and that a wife should be a help-meet and partner to her spouse, not a servant to be ordered about." He paused and shrugged. "That was one of the lessons my father drummed into my head. I remember him and my mother arguing vociferously once and when I questioned him, he explained that he had failed to respect her. That has always stuck in my mind as one of his most powerful lessons to me."

Elizabeth nodded and looked Darcy in the eye. "I am glad he spoke of it to you." She glanced down. "The example I have had before me daily in the form of my parents' marriage is not one of mutual respect. I have no wish to live in that manner. Thank you for your reassurances."

Darcy only smiled at her and nodded.

Chapter 5

Later that afternoon, after Darcy had gone and Annabelle's at-home hours had ended, Somerset knocked on Blackwell's study door, where he had been attending to some correspondence.

"Come."

The wood panel opened and the butler entered, his features pinched.

"Sir Augustus Perry wishes to see you, sir."

Blackwell had been informed of the baron's actions with Elizabeth that morning and was surprised to find the man wanting a word with him now. His lips flattened.

"I wonder what he wants." He shook his head. "Bring him in but do not bring refreshments. Have Wood and Stopford stationed outside the door to this room. They should be prepared to throw the baron out if it is required."

Somerset nodded, his stiff posture relaxing. "As you wish."

A few minutes later, the butler knocked again, this time opening the door and announcing the visitor.

"Thank you for seeing me, Blackwell." Sir Augustus bowed, a grin that could only be described as smug lifting his lips.

Blackwell's mouth turned down at the corners. He gestured to one of the chairs in front of his desk. "Have a seat." As the two of them settled in, he rested his elbows on the arms of his chair, holding his hands in front of him in the shape of a steeple. "What can I do for you?"

Sir Augustus' smirk faded slowly away. He shifted. "I can see you have no desire to beat about the bush, as you have neither offered me a drink nor inquired after my health. Therefore, I will simply state my reasons for calling upon you."

Blackwell said nothing, only staring at the baron over his joined hands.

Clearing his throat, the gentleman began. "I understand that Miss Elizabeth has accepted an offer of marriage from Mr. Darcy. I am here to persuade you against accepting his suit and instead consenting to mine." Augustus waved a hand to the right. "I have long desired to make your niece my wife. A scandal being attached to her name does not affect those desires in the least. My fortune is ample to support her and any children we might have."

Blackwell brought his hands, at which he had been staring while the baron made his speech, down from in front of his face. "Well, sir, there is nothing you have said that cannot be applied to Mr. Darcy, whose name is the one linked with my niece's in the scandal you mentioned. You will have to do better than that to persuade me against him."

Augustus began to bluster. "You well know that your niece has no fortune whatsoever. If

48

not for what happened at the ball last night, she would never have had an offer from him or anyone of his ilk. As I understand it, her mother is unsuitable. Darcy may turn away from her for that and reject her. Worse, he may mistreat her because of her connections. Elizabeth will never receive a better offer than what I have given her. I am in a position where I can overlook her unfortunate relations, as well as her lack of fortune."

Blackwell sat in silence for a moment, trying to calm his anger. Finally, he stood. "As you are well aware, my niece rejected your request for a courtship last week. This morning, she refused your offer of marriage. You apparently do not feel she is serious, because here you are, asking me to rebuff an eminently suitable mate for her while at the same time insulting her and all my family. No, sir, I will not trade Darcy's suit for yours. Elizabeth will become Mrs. Darcy and you will look elsewhere for a baroness." He strode around the desk and the open-mouthed Sir Augustus, stopping at the hallway door. "You are to leave my home, now, never to return. I intend to inform the staff that you are no longer welcome in this house. If you accost any of my family members, including my niece, while we are out in public, you will receive the cut direct." He held up a hand when the other man began to speak. "You may have a title, but my family is an old and well-respected one. Our status in society is well-established and our coffers are full. We have no need of anything you could possibly bring to us." He opened the door. "Good day, sir."

Instantly, Somerset appeared, flanked by Wood and Stopford.

Sir Augustus looked at the men facing him and snarled. "You will regret this, I promise you." Then, he pushed his way past his host and marched down the hall, the servants on his heels.

James shut the door then, shaking his head as his shoulders briefly dropped. He walked to the window and watched as the baron almost leaped off the front steps, shaking his fist and shouting up at his driver. "No, sir, I will not regret it, and neither will my niece."

~~~***~~~

The next day, Darcy arrived at the Blackwell home with his friend Bingley in tow. The pair bowed to Annabelle, Jane, and Elizabeth when they entered.

"I hope you do not mind our visit. Blackwell indicated I would always be welcome." Darcy gestured to his friend. "When Bingley discovered where I was going, he expressed an interest in seeing Miss Bennet again, so I brought him along."

"We do not mind at all, do we girls?" Annabelle smiled as she gestured to the seating area. "Please do come join us. We just ordered tea. I will have them add more cups to the tray."

"Thank you." Darcy and his friend made their way to the girls and sat, each at the side of his preferred Bennet, while Annabelle went to pull the bell and then gave instructions to the maid who responded to her summons.

"How are you today, Miss Elizabeth?" Darcy settled into the seat, laying his arm across the high back of the piece.

Elizabeth smiled. "I am well." She nodded toward Jane, whose blush had overspread her features even as her smile remained serene. "Thank you for bringing your friend with you. My sister has had nothing but good to say of him."

"He has had nothing but praise for her." Darcy watched the couple closely. "It is good to know that their admiration is mutual."

"It is." Elizabeth clasped her hands in her lap, looking at Jane and Bingley with a small smile playing over her lips. She turned to Darcy. "Jane is difficult to read, but there is a twinkle in her eye when she looks at him that I have never seen before. Add that to the way she turns red when in his presence and I deduce she is well on her way to being in love."

Darcy's brows rose. "Such subtle signs."

Elizabeth shrugged. "That is her way. She shows a serene face to the world but she has a tender heart. She does not want everyone to know what she is thinking or feeling. When you meet my mother, you will understand why she does this."

Darcy's brow creased as he contemplated her words. He wondered if Mrs. Bennet was not every bit as badly behaved as her family seemed to let on. He supposed he would find out soon enough. Instead of asking more about her mother, he spoke of himself. "It has been said of me that I am reserved. My sister has, on more than one occasion, accused me of being unfeeling because of it. I suppose Miss Bennet is perfectly capable of letting my friend know how she feels, and I must leave them to work out a relationship themselves, no matter what form it eventually takes."

"You must. It does no one any good for others to meddle in their lives. Look what happened with us." Elizabeth's arms came up to cross over her chest. Her brow rose, and Darcy could see the challenge in her demeanor.

He rushed to reassure her. "I meant no disrespect. Bingley is modest and relies on my judgement a great deal. He is a good friend. An excellent one, actually, and I know he will call upon me to give my opinion. I only wished to be certain of what I should say to him." He was relieved when Elizabeth's arms came down.

"I suppose I cannot blame you for that," she conceded as she examined him, a corner of her lips turned down. "Forgive me," she said, smoothing her features. "I replied to your question but did not bother to reciprocate. How are you?"

Darcy tipped his head to her. "I am well. My

business with my uncle was easily accomplished. By this time next week, we will have a special license and may marry at the time and place of our choosing."

"Good." Elizabeth looked away for just a moment, biting her lip. "I remember you said the archbishop is a relative of yours ... your uncle?" She waited for her companion to nod. "Did he have anything to say?"

Darcy shrugged. "He asked me details of the incident at Westerville's ball, but once I assured him of your innocence – as well as my own – and made him understand the excellence of your character, he was happy to accept my application."

Elizabeth smirked. "But, sir, how well do you really know my character? We were not introduced before our unfortunate incident."

"We were not," Darcy conceded. The corner of his lip lifted the smallest bit. "However, I have been assured by your uncle, as well as by your behavior and that of the rest of your family, that you are all that is good and kind. Had you been out to trap me, your face would not have been perpetually tear-stained the last two days." He reached a finger out to trace gently down her cheek from her eye to her chin. "I can see the redness about your eyes that tells me you have been at it again today."

She blushed and looked down at her hands. She pressed her lips together for a moment and then, with a sigh, lifted her chin. "I have,

53

yes. I am not formed for melancholy, however, and am endeavoring to see the good in the situation."

Darcy lifted one corner of his lips into a half-smile. "As am I." He drained the last of the tea in his cup. "I visited another uncle this morning, as well."

Elizabeth's brows rose. "Which one is this?"

"My mother's brother, Lord Henry Fitzwilliam, Earl of Matlock. He had heard the gossip from his wife, who had seen it in the papers. He questioned me closely about the event."

She tilted her head and chewed her lip as she examined his mien. "Did he attempt to dissuade you?"

Darcy shrugged. "I confess he did. I will not go into the arguments he made, but they were nothing less than I expected. However, in the end he came to the understanding that we were both innocent victims and that I am firm in my desire to repair both of our reputations by marrying you. He has given his blessing, though I did not ask for or require it."

"Still, to have it will ..."

Their attention was caught at that moment by Mr. Bingley, who had been speaking to Annabelle. "I would like to invite you all to dine with me on Monday. My eldest sister and her husband will be out with friends, but my youngest sister will be my hostess."

"I believe we are free that evening." Annabelle

paused. "Are you certain your sister will not mind hosting us, given the circumstances?"

Bingley shrugged. "She may mind or not mind, but I have issued the invitation and she will behave as she should or she may find herself in her own establishment." His countenance took on an unusually solemn, for him, demeanor. "I assume she will have heard the gossip by then, but it is my home and my table, and I know what really happened at that ball. I will have whomever I wish to dine with me." He paused. "I should, perhaps, not share so many private details, but Caroline has been spoiled all her life, first by my parents and then, because I did not know better, by me. I have recently realized that if I do not take charge of her, she will spend the rest of time arranging my life, possibly in ways I do not relish living. The thought makes me shudder. I have been pushing her to find a husband this year. It is her second season." He sat back. "Anyway, if she objects, she can find a new place to live. I want you to come and that is all that matters."

Annabelle pressed her hand to her chest. "Oh, my." She looked at Elizabeth and Jane, who both smiled at her. "Very well, then. I will check with Mr. Blackwell before you leave, just to make sure, but I happily accept your kind invitation."

"Excellent!" Bingley beamed. "Darcy, you are invited, as well; it should go without saying."

Darcy smirked. "Indeed. I will be happy to attend. Thank you for the invitation."

"Bring Georgiana, if you can."

Elizabeth's brows furrowed and then released as she tilted her head. "Georgiana is your sister? You mentioned before that you had one but we did not have the opportunity for me to ask."

"Georgiana is my sister. She is four and ten and still in school." Darcy turned his attention back to his friend. "Unfortunately, I will not see her before your dinner, but I thank you for including her."

Bingley frowned. "That is too bad. She is a lovely girl." He looked at Jane. "I think you and Miss Elizabeth would like her very much."

Jane smiled. "I am certain we would. We very much enjoy making new acquaintances."

Elizabeth turned everyone's attention back to Darcy by asking for more information. "She is much younger than you if she is just four and ten, is she not? Does she look like you?"

"She is more than ten years my junior. She looks like my mother but with my father's height. She is blonde and blue-eyed, much like Miss Bennet." He nodded toward Jane. "She excels in music; she practices the pianoforte almost constantly when she is at home. She is shy, though, and rarely performs for others. I have told her that she will be required to exhibit once she comes out in three or four years, but for now, I am content to keep her talents to myself."

Elizabeth grinned. "Such a kind older brother you are. I suspect you do not at all mind being the sole recipient of her attention in this area."

Darcy smirked. He found that he enjoyed the twinkle that appeared in his betrothed's eyes as she teased him. "Georgiana has said the same to me. I freely admit that I do not wish to lose her company. We are very close. We were even before my father passed away four years ago, but me being her primary guardian has drawn us even more so." He shrugged. "It has been just the two of us for a long time. We have grown to depend upon each other."

Elizabeth's gaze softened. "I can see how that would happen. I am glad you have had each other."

The newly betrothed couple stared into each other's eyes for a long minute. The moment was soon broken, however, by the resumption of conversation amongst the rest of the party.

Chapter 6

After a lengthy visit with Elizabeth and her family, Darcy and Bingley boarded the former's carriage to return to Darcy House. Bingley immediately, as was his wont, began a conversation. He cocked his head and looked Darcy up and down.

"Miss Elizabeth is a very nice young lady."

"She is. Or at least, she has been so far." Darcy shrugged. "It matters not either way at this point, but I believe I have accurately sketched her character."

"I suspect you have. We have not had much opportunity to talk the last couple days; allow me to now inquire what your feelings are about the events of the last eight and forty hours or so."

Darcy sighed. "At first, I was angry. I have never responded well to being forced to do anything, as you know."

Bingley nodded and chuckled. "That, I do. But, you were only angry at first?"

Darcy smirked but then became serious again. "Yes, just at first." He sighed. "I do not know if I can explain it well, but ... I find myself attracted to Miss Elizabeth. Her tears at the ball struck me as sincere and her initial vehement insistence that we not marry made me realize that she either did not know about my fortune or did not care. There were no inquiries about me or my estate. None at all, not even after I assured her that I could well take care of her. It was refreshing, to be honest."

"I would imagine it was." Bingley grinned. "That is not something an eligible gentleman of fortune often experiences, is it?"

Darcy shook his head. "No, it is not." He paused. "Anyway, that is part of her attraction. I am physically attracted, as well. She is a beautiful woman." He shrugged. "I will not say more, except to relate that the longer I know her, the more I feel that marriage to her is the correct step to take. It goes beyond doing my duty, which is how it began. I simply feel in my soul that this is what I am meant to do."

"That must make it easier to bear."

"It does." Darcy raised his brow at his friend. "And what about you? I see you have found another angel in Miss Bennet."

Bingley grinned. "I have, have I not? She is the most beautiful creature I have ever beheld, and I think she likes me."

Darcy smiled. "Her sister seems to think she does. Miss Elizabeth tells me Miss Bennet is reserved but that there is a twinkle in her eye when she is with you that has never been observed in her before. She does blush when you speak to her." He shook his head to see Bingley puff out his chest a bit. "She is being spoken of very poorly, though I would imagine her sister's marriage to me will make the gossip disappear immediately. A married couple is far less interesting to gossip about than an unmarried one."

Bingley shrugged. "As I said to the ladies, I was at that ball and I know what happened. I do not consider anyone involved to be ruined. I admire Miss Bennet. I have since I first met her. It is my desire to get to know her better."

"How much better?" Darcy tilted his head and watched his friend.

Bingley looked the other gentleman in the eye. "I can see myself married to her. Once we become better acquainted, I plan to propose, unless she reveals herself to be hideous."

"What of Caroline?"

Bingley shrugged again. "She can mind her own business. She is not married now because of her own ridiculously high standards. She cannot blame any future lack of suitors on my connection to the sister of an unfairly accused woman."

Darcy grinned. "I am happy to hear you say that. I remain impressed with your sternness toward her."

Bingley rolled his eyes. "It took me long enough to see through her machinations, you mean. I apologize to you again; I had no idea she would attempt to force her attentions on to you like she did." He shook his head. "My sanctions appear to have changed her attitude. I do not wish to lose your friendship because Caroline keeps throwing herself at your head."

"I would not wish to lose yours, either. I appreciate the steps you have taken. They are the reason I accepted your invitation to dinner."

"I thought as much." Bingley smiled. "She will be angry that you are out of her reach now, but she will behave as a perfect lady while there are guests in the house. She does not want to form her own establishment and have to live off only the interest from her fortune."

Now it was Darcy's turn to roll his eyes. "She may argue with you about Miss Bennet, you know."

Bingley nodded. "I do know, but anything she says will go in one ear and out the other. It is my life and my marriage and I do not want her in the middle of it. I will pay court to whatever woman I wish to. Caroline should count her blessings that I did not choose the scullery maid."

Darcy laughed out loud. "Indeed."

~~~***~~~

Over the course of the following days, Darcy made daily visits to see Elizabeth. He dined with the Blackwells every evening, and attended church with them on Sunday, making it plain by his actions that he was attached to her. He made the most of each visit to get to know his betrothed better.

On one such call, the two were playing chess when he struck up a conversation.

"What do you think of books, Miss Elizabeth?" Darcy moved the piece on the board in front of him and looked up to see her face.

"I love to read." Elizabeth flashed him a smile and then turned her attention to the game, a crease forming between her brows. Finally, she picked up a pawn and moved it. "Do you? You must, or you would not have asked me." She sat back in her chair.

"I confess I do. I inherited two large libraries, one in my home here in town and one at Pemberley, and I have made it a bit of a mission to add to each of them." He paused to decide which piece to move, then chose to mirror her maneuver with his own pawn. He looked up. "Do you have a favorite author?"

"I love to laugh, so Shakespeare's comedies are my favorites. However, I will read almost anything. I have often read philosophy and debated it with my father. I read poetry quite a bit. I find history fascinating; I especially love to read about how people in the past lived."

Darcy nodded. "Shakespeare is a favorite of mine, as well, and I also read history and poetry. I was forced to read the great philosophers at University and I confess I was happy to leave them behind. I understood what I read and am perfectly able to debate anyone about them, but they do not hold my interest like a good historical analysis does."

Elizabeth smiled. "I can understand that. Jane is well-read, too, and feels as you do about philosophy. She prefers novels. She says she reads for the adventure of it, not to learn." She giggled. "She says serious reading and the thinking that goes along with it makes her head ache."

Darcy chuckled and glanced across the room to where Bingley and Jane were engaged in a quiet conversation. "She will get along well with my friend, then. He is of a similar mind. He does not enjoy reading much at all, though he is perfectly capable of the exercise." He shook his head. "I cannot understand not being able to lose oneself in a good book."

"I cannot, either." She lifted a shoulder as she moved her next piece. "I do like a good novel. They are a great way to escape the humdrum reality of life. But to never read anything deeper would bore me to tears, I think." She looked up. "Do you read novels?"

"I have, yes. I often read the ones my sister has expressed an interest in, to assure myself of their content before I allow her to have them." His eyes focused on his remaining pieces. Elizabeth had swept away many of his pawns and a couple knights. "As a rule, I enjoy them, but like you, I would not want to make a steady diet of them." He made his move and then sat back and watched in silent shock as his betrothed swept her piece in and took his queen.

"Checkmate." Elizabeth's eyes lit up, her countenance glowing in her victory.

Darcy found his voice as he took in her expression. "Congratulations." He could not look away. He found her enticing in the extreme when she looked as she did, and his heart skipped a beat before taking up a much harder rhythm than it had before.

"Thank you, sir. Would you like to play again? Perhaps this time I might let you win?" She laughed before giving him an impertinent grin.

Darcy could not resist smiling in return. "I would like to play another game. Perhaps this time I might not let you win." He winked and grinned at her blush.

On another visit, he and Elizabeth were sitting together in front of the fire, sharing a sofa, when she made an inquiry of him.

"Tell me, Mr. Darcy ... what amusements do you enjoy? What are your accomplishments, aside from startling unsuspecting young ladies into leaping at you?" Her tone of voice and raised brow made it clear she was teasing.

"Well," he began after thinking about it for a moment, "you already know I enjoy reading." He looked at her and when she nodded, he continued. "I derive at least as much pleasure from riding. I go out on one of my horses every day the weather allows."

"I saw that you rode today instead of bringing your carriage."

"I did. The weather is very fine and I saw no reason to stuff myself inside of an equipage when I could be out enjoying the sunshine."

Darcy sipped the tea from the cup he had been holding.

"It is rather cold, though." Elizabeth's eyes twinkled as her lips twitched.

"Yes," he conceded. "It was rather cold, but I dressed warmly. I suffered no ill effects. I do not mind being cold." He shrugged. "I often find myself overly warm when inside."

Elizabeth nodded. "My father is like that. Mama fusses at him incessantly in the winter for going out and about in the cold."

Darcy grinned. "I take after my father, and I well remember my mother doing the same to him."

"Oh, my. I wonder if I will do likewise to you." She laughed.

Darcy found that he loved to hear her laughter. It was a warm gurgling sound as opposed to the high-pitched tinkling of most of the ladies he knew. He forced his attention back to her words and away from his desire to stop her laugh with his lips.

"What other accomplishments do you claim?" She tilted her head as she looked at him.

"My mother was a gifted musician. She taught me to play the pianoforte when I was a child. I did not keep up with it after her death, but I am still capable of playing simple tunes. So, I can add 'pianoforte player' to my list." He blushed at his confession, but her expression of delighted surprise made him happy he had shared it.

"How wonderful! My mother does not play, and neither does Jane, but I learned a little and my next sister, Mary, practices constantly."

"Perhaps you would play for me some evening. I would love to hear you."

She shrugged. "Perhaps." Her eyes rolled. "I am quite certain I will be forced to one of these days. My aunts were teasing me about it yesterday, and I expect one or the other will make me play after dinner one night soon."

"I look forward to it." He paused. "What other accomplishments do you claim?"

"Oh, I have a few." She sat her cup on the table beside her and turned so that she was better able to face him. "I sew – embroidery mostly, but I can also hem a gown and apply lace to it. I enjoy making items for the tenants ... baby items, and aprons, mostly.

"I have already told you that I love to read. I have painted a screen, but I confess I am not very good at it. My favorite activity is walking. I miss it when I am here. I am allowed to go into Hyde Park if I wish, but I have to take a maid and a footman with me and that slows me down, so I only go now and then."

Darcy smiled at her enthusiasm. "Do you ride?"

"I know how, but it is not a favored activity. My father does not keep many horses. We have the two for the carriage that also work the farm, and we have my father's gelding and our old mare, Nellie." She shook her head. "It was easier to get out of the house to walk than it was to get a horse to ride, and I am capable of walking much faster than Nellie is, so I came to prefer walking. I love my walks … they are time I have totally to myself that I can use to ponder the things that are happening in my life."

Darcy nodded slowly. "I can understand that. I use my riding time for the same purpose."

Elizabeth's smile at his words warmed his heart. "You do understand, then. Not many can."

He resisted the urge to reach his hand out to cover hers where it rested in her lap. He had a very good feeling about their relationship.

Chapter 7

Finally, Monday came and with it the dinner at Bingley's townhouse. Darcy escorted Elizabeth and Annabelle in his carriage, with Jane and her uncle following in the Blackwells' equipage. The five of them entered the house to find Bingley bouncing on his toes, a happy smile on his face.

"Welcome! Welcome! So good of you all to come tonight."

Darcy shook his head at his friend. "I see you are eager for the evening to begin. Have you been waiting in the foyer all afternoon?"

Bingley laughed. "I have!" He suddenly stopped moving and put his fists on his hips. "I thought you would never get here. I was about to wither away to nothing!"

Their host's behavior put Elizabeth and her relatives at ease, and they were soon laughing as they followed him down the hall to the drawing room.

"Come in, come in." Bingley waved them into the room. "Allow me to introduce my sister to you." He approached the thin, well-dressed woman with similar coloring to his that stood in front of the sofa.

"This is Miss Caroline Bingley, the younger of my two sisters. Caroline, you already know Darcy. The gentleman with him is Mr. James

Blackwell of Black Manor in Wiltshire and
Bruton Street here in London, and his wife,
Mrs. Blackwell. With him also are his nieces,
Miss Jane Bennet and Miss Elizabeth Bennet,
of Longbourn in Hertfordshire."

Once the requisite bows and curtseys had
been exchanged, Bingley invited everyone to
sit, and they all obliged him.

"You have a very fine house here, Miss
Bingley."

Elizabeth's eyes involuntarily gazed about
the room at her aunt's polite compliment to
their hostess. The furnishings were very fine,
indeed, but it was clearly the over-decorated
house of someone who wished to show off her
wealth. She suppressed a shiver. She much
preferred her aunt's tasteful and understated
decorations. She happened to catch Darcy's
eye as she returned her attention to Miss
Bingley and noted one of his brows lift. She
rolled her eyes and saw a corner of his lips
twitch in a quick smirk.

The butler interrupted whatever might have
been said next to announce another guest.

"Colonel Richard Fitzwilliam."

"Oh, Darcy, I forgot to tell you … I invited
your cousin to make up the numbers." Bingley
turned to the colonel. "Come in, Fitzwilliam.
Let me introduce you to the other guests."

Within just a few moments, the introductions
had been made and everyone resumed their
places. The colonel sat in a chair near the settee

on which Darcy and Elizabeth were seated.

"I am happy to make your acquaintance, Miss Elizabeth." The colonel glanced at Darcy. "My father told me of your betrothal. I have seen neither hide nor hair of Darcy in days, so I was not able to ask him about it."

Elizabeth's forehead creased as she turned to her betrothed.

"Colonel Fitzwilliam is my cousin on my mother's side. He is Lord Matlock's second son and my sister's other guardian."

"Lord Matlock is the uncle you mentioned the other day?"

Darcy nodded. "It is."

Elizabeth smiled and turned to the colonel. "I am happy to meet you, as well."

"Father told me he gave Darcy a hard time about your engagement. Let me apologize on his behalf. He is a stickler for the old ways, including marrying with status in mind, and is very much stuck in his ways." The colonel held his hands out at his sides, palms up. "He sometimes accuses me and my cousin here of being too honest. He means well; he simply cannot see any perspective but his own."

Elizabeth's head moved slowly up and down. "I see. Will he give me trouble, then, despite the blessing he gave Mr. Darcy?" She felt her betrothed touch her arm and looked at him.

"Fear not. I will not allow him to disparage or mistreat you. You will be Mrs. Darcy; disrespect is not tolerated." His intense gaze drilled into her eyes.

"Thank you." She lifted her lips in a small smile. "I appreciate your reassurances." She turned her attention back to the colonel. "I have heard much from Mr. Darcy about himself, his likes and his dislikes. What can you tell me about him?" She smirked. "I would imagine your view of him is quite different than his of himself."

Fitzwilliam laughed and proceeded to spend the next quarter hour regaling Elizabeth with stories of Darcy from his youth. The rest of the party was soon listening, and the time passed with a great deal of laughter, including from the groom-to-be.

It did not take long for everyone in the party to understand that Caroline Bingley was hosting the dinner under duress. She was the only one who did not laugh at Fitzwilliam's stories, and she literally looked down her nose at the guests, especially the ladies.

When the meal was announced and Darcy escorted Elizabeth into the dining room, he was unsurprised to see that Caroline's displeasure was extended to seating during the meal. She had resorted to elegantly scripted cards in front of the place settings to indicate who was to sit where. He whispered an apology to his betrothed as he walked her around the table to her assigned seat at the far end.

"I am sorry for this. We should have been

seated closer together."

Elizabeth squeezed his arm. "All is well. I am between my uncle and your friend, and I find both of them to be amiable gentlemen of good conversation." She paused. "I am sorry, though, that you are seated next to Miss Bingley. She does not appear to be very happy to be hosting us."

"I doubt she is." Darcy glanced toward Caroline when he heard her clear her throat. "But I trust Bingley to keep her under control." He smiled and squeezed Elizabeth's hand, then moved to take his place. He looked at his hostess again and felt the mask of indifference that he used in social situations descend upon his features.

Once all the ladies were seated, the gentlemen followed, and Caroline gestured to the servants to begin serving. Darcy had been correct in his words to Elizabeth: Caroline Bingley was supremely unhappy to be hosting this dinner.

She looked to her right, where the object of her matrimonial hopes was seated. She had become enraged when her brother informed her of Darcy's engagement. It was unexpected, to say the least. She knew he had not been courting anyone and could not comprehend how he could have been snatched up under her nose like that.

Caroline did not learn of the circumstances of Darcy's betrothal from her brother. She had attended a different ball with her sister and brother-in-law that fateful night. She heard the gossip the next day, though, as it made the rounds from house to house. She had been horrified. She sniffed at the thought of *her* Darcy being captured by such an infamous female. She turned her gaze down the table and narrowed her eyes at Elizabeth, who had turned her head toward Charles to speak. *Insufferable trollop,* she thought.

Next, she turned her attention toward Jane Bennet, who had clearly gained her brother's attention. *Another insufferable trollop. It is ridiculous that I must play hostess to such people.* She allowed the conversation on either side of her to carry on without her input as she considered her guests. *I cannot have that woman join my family, nor can I allow her nasty sister to usurp my future position as the mistress of Pemberley. My brother and his friend must be separated from these women,* she thought. *But how?* She did not have time just then to formulate a plan, as she had to attend to her duties, but she vowed to come up with something before she went to sleep that night.

As per custom, once the meal was finished, the ladies separated from the gentlemen and retired to the drawing room. Caroline led the way, gritting her teeth at being forced to entertain such people all alone.

Once in the drawing room, she invited the ladies to sit and began a conversation with

Annabelle that led to the trio of guests discussing something among themselves, allowing Caroline to evaluate Elizabeth and silently formulate a plan of action. She was determined to finish the ruination of the undeserving chit that was begun at the Westerville ball.

Elizabeth, her sister, and her aunt made several attempts to draw their hostess into their conversation, but Caroline simply sat, stiff and cold, and made no more than monosyllabic responses. She saw them shrug to themselves and was relieved when they carried on without further input from her. She was certain they were as delighted as she was when the gentlemen finally joined them.

~~~***~~~

The next morning, Elizabeth and her sister found themselves alone in the family parlor upstairs in their aunt and uncle's house. Mr. Blackwell had gone out for an appointment and their aunt was meeting with the housekeeper.

"Lizzy?"

Elizabeth looked up from her book. "Yes?"

Jane bit her lip, and Elizabeth could tell she was uncertain how to word whatever it was she was about to say. Finally, with a sigh, she lifted her eyes from her needlework and gazed into her sister's similar orbs. "I do not wish to stir up feelings which would be better left buried, but ... you have not spoken about what happened to you in days. How do you really feel?" She set her embroidery hoop aside and moved from the chair nearest the window to the settee where Elizabeth was sitting. "Are you certain you are willing to marry Mr. Darcy?"

Elizabeth stilled and then closed the book, marking her page with a piece of ribbon. She placed the tome in her lap and turned to face her sister. She opened her mouth, closed it again, and then finally found the words to say.

"I believe I have made my peace with it. It is not Mr. Darcy's fault we are in this position. It is not mine, either, and I know that I am ..." She paused, searching for the correct term. "I am saving the reputations of not only myself but of you and our other sisters, as well." She reached out to grasp Jane's hand. "In a way, I am doing my duty."

Jane hesitated. "Do you like him?"

"Mr. Darcy?" When her sister nodded, Elizabeth pulled her lips between her teeth and looked down. Finally, she said, "I do, actually. He is very handsome and kind, and he has promised to respect me and my opinions. Though it has only been a week that we have been engaged, he has never once displayed contempt at any opinion I have given. I have high hopes that he will continue and not suddenly turn into someone else. Uncle has assured me that he is a man of honor." She shrugged and looked at Jane. "I feel strange things when he is near."

Jane's brow creased. "What do you mean, 'strange things'?"

Elizabeth shook her head as her forehead wrinkled. "I do not know if I can explain it. When he touches me, I feel a sort of tingle where ever his hand comes into contact with me. Then, when he first enters a room after being absent from it for a while, and I hear his voice, it is as though my heart stops beating for just a second or two. I feel a thrill go through me when he addresses me." She blushed and looked back down, shrugging. "I do not know if I am explaining it well or if it even makes sense."

"It makes perfect sense to me." Jane touched her sister's hand, and Elizabeth looked up at her to see the older girl's lips lifted in a small smile. "I feel similar things when I am with Mr. Bingley." She paused. "Do you think you might be in love with him?"

Elizabeth shook her head. "I do not see how that is possible after so short an acquaintance. Infatuated, perhaps. I own to that possibility." She hesitated. "I believe I am attracted to him, as a woman to a man." She reddened. "I should probably not admit that even to you."

Jane smiled and tilted her head. "I am glad you have. I should think it would be important, given that you are marrying him and will have to kiss him."

Elizabeth rolled her eyes but chuckled. "I suppose you are correct."

"Of course I am!" Jane sat back and grinned. "When have I ever been wrong?" She winked when Elizabeth burst out laughing.

Chapter 8

Two days later, the ladies of the Blackwell household went out to the shops. Annabelle had made an appointment for Elizabeth with her modiste and the day had come for the bridal shopping to begin.

With the events of the previous week in mind, Annabelle had made the appointment for early in the day. It was so early that there were few people out at all, and definitely none of the upper ten-thousand, who were all at home sleeping off the events of the night before. Therefore, they were not subjected to any rude behavior.

Madam Claire had been Annabelle's choice of modiste for over three decades, and the dressmaker both liked her customer and valued her business. After the lady's previous visit, when the girls had been rude, she had stressed to her seamstresses and assistant that Mrs. Blackwell and anyone she chose to bring with her to the shop were to be treated as the treasured customers they were. Any girl who behaved inappropriately would be immediately dismissed. This warning ensured that Elizabeth and her sister were treated with care and respect despite the rumors that abounded about them.

By the time the ladies were finished with

the modiste, they had worked up a craving for tea and pastries. They decided to walk across the street to their favorite tea shop and partake, rather than go to a more popular place further down.

Though their plan was a good one, the day had lengthened to the point that the streets were far more crowded than they had been when they arrived. They looked at each other, and Elizabeth bit her lip, but the trio lifted their chins and allowed the footman to escort them across the street.

When they entered the shop, they found most of the tables filled. The sound of the chatter was loud, but the volume began to lower as the family made their way to the nearest open table. They seated themselves, and the noise began to slowly increase again, but the tone of it changed.

Elizabeth felt as though every eye in the place was on her, and she did not like it. Her spine stiffened as her courage rose. She looked around, meeting the eye of any who would look her way.

"Are you well, my dear?" Annabelle whispered her question as she patted Elizabeth's hand. "We can leave if you wish."

"No." Elizabeth shook her head. "I have no wish to leave. If anyone does not want to visit this shop when I am here, they may leave." She lifted the corners of her lips in an attempt to smile.

"Then we shall stay." Annabelle flashed a

bright grin at both of her nieces before giving their order to the proprietor.

After that, the three ladies simply conversed among themselves and enjoyed their tea and scones. They noticed the others skirting around them, but paid no one else any mind. When they were finished, they rose.

As they approached the door, it opened again to reveal Caroline Bingley and another woman stepping inside. Elizabeth was in front of her aunt, and Jane was behind her. When Caroline looked up and saw who stood before her, she froze for a moment. Elizabeth began to curtsey and opened her mouth to greet her; Caroline lifted her nose in the air and turned away without acknowledging the ladies in front of her.

Elizabeth froze, shock coursing through her. She could hear the welcome Miss Bingley was receiving from other customers. Suddenly, she heard her aunt whispering behind her.

"Walk forward, Lizzy. Pretend like nothing happened."

With a lift of her chin and a stiffened posture, Elizabeth obeyed her aunt's command. Once outside, she was surrounded on one side by Jane and the other by Annabelle. They took her arms and silently crossed to their waiting carriage, where they boarded and Mrs. Blackwell ordered the driver to take them home.

Inside, as the equipage lurched into motion, Elizabeth sat with her jaw clenched. Jane was rubbing one of her hands; the other was curled into a fist.

"I am so sorry, Lizzy," Annabelle said, shaking her head. "We did so well. There was clearly talk, but no one behaved poorly until that tradesman's daughter gave you the cut direct. Who does she think she is?"

Elizabeth swallowed hard. "Apparently, she thinks she is better than me." She took a deep breath. "Nothing like that has ever happened to me before." She closed her eyes. "Would that it had not happened now."

Annabelle leaned across the carriage and took her niece's free hand. "I am sorry, dear. My heart breaks for you. You have always been the epitome of propriety and grace. To see you treated thusly when you have been falsely accused makes me want to shake my fist at the heavens."

Elizabeth wiped the tears that had started trickling down her cheeks. "Thank you for your support." She swallowed back more tears and took in another deep breath. "Hopefully, my marriage puts all of this to rest. Though, I do not know that I ever want to participate in society if this is how they behave."

Jane wiped her sister's eyes with her handkerchief. "I do not blame you, Lizzy. But, please, do not allow yourself to become bitter about this. You must forgive them. You know what Mary always says."

Elizabeth sniffed and nodded. "I do."

Annabelle's brows lifted. "What does Mary say?"

"That forgiveness is for us and not for the person who wronged us. We must forgive those who spitefully use us, even when they do not come to us and ask for it. We cannot expect our Savior to forgive us if we do not forgive others." Jane lifted a shoulder. "It is an easy precept to follow most of the time."

"But most of the time, our reputations are not totally ruined." This time, even Elizabeth could hear the bitterness in her voice. "I am sorry," she said, turning her face toward the window.

The other ladies in the carriage said nothing. The three of them rode the rest of the way to Bruton Street in silence.

~~~***~~~

That evening, the Blackwells and their nieces were to attend a dinner at Darcy House. Elizabeth had spent the day in her chambers with a cold cloth on her aching head. She had assured her sister and aunt that it was likely caused by the distress of the morning and they had left her alone. She had considered asking her uncle to send a note to Darcy, cancelling their attendance, but she knew the meal was a special event and that his staff would have had extra work added to their daily tasks to make it happen. Despite her deepest wishes, she could not in good conscience ask them to go to all that trouble for nothing. No, she would rest as long as she could and then she would dress and go.

Darcy was waiting for his guests in the foyer of his home. He saw immediately that his betrothed was not herself. After bowing to the company, he reached for Elizabeth's hand. "Are you well?"

Elizabeth shrugged. "I will be." She lifted her lips in a weak imitation of her usual sunny smile.

"What has happened?" Darcy looked with concern at Elizabeth first, but then his gaze travelled from one of her family members to another.

Blackwell tipped his head in the direction of a nearby doorway. "Perhaps we can discuss it in a more private location?"

"Certainly." Darcy immediately tucked Elizabeth's hand under his arm and escorted her down the hall to the drawing room. Once there, he invited the group to sit as he maneuvered his betrothed to a sofa, seated her, and took his place beside her.

"Now," he said, "tell me what has happened."

The tale of the morning's venture was soon shared. Darcy stood up in the middle of the retelling to pace. He felt the blood pounding in his ears. He clenched both his jaw and his fists, hoping to stem the tide of his anger before it exploded. When he was sure he had control of himself, he stopped pacing and addressed his betrothed.

"I am so sorry, Elizabeth. Would that I could take the pain away. I promise you-" His words were cut off when the butler entered and announced more guests.

"Lord and Lady Matlock, Colonel Fitzwilliam, and Mr. Bingley." Mr. Baxter stepped to the side so the visitors could enter, then turned toward the entrance to the room. He paused to allow Darcy's sister to come in, giving her an affectionate smile, and once she was inside, closed the door.

Darcy began making introductions, his tone of voice rather clipped.

"Aunt, Uncle, this is Mr. James Blackwell and his wife. You may know Blackwell from the club."

"Indeed, I do. Pleased to see you, Blackwell." Lord Matlock inclined his head as James bowed to him.

"Mr. and Mrs. Blackwell, this is my uncle, the Earl of Matlock, and my aunt, Viscountess Matlock."

Lady Matlock gestured to the Bennet girls. "Which of these lovely ladies is your betrothed?"

"These are the Bennets." Darcy indicated Jane first. "Miss Jane Bennet, and ..." He grasped Elizabeth's hand. "My betrothed, Miss Elizabeth Bennet."

Elizabeth and Jane curtseyed and murmured greetings to the newcomers.

Darcy continued the introductions. "You have all met my cousin and Bingley."

More greetings were spoken and bows and curtseys given.

"This ..." He gestured to the young girl at the back of the group, beckoning her forward. "Is my sister, Miss Georgiana Darcy. Georgiana, this is Mr. and Mrs. Blackwell, Miss Jane Bennet, and your soon-to-be sister, Miss Elizabeth Bennet."

Georgiana blushed at being the center of attention. "I am happy to meet you all."

Elizabeth smiled warmly. "I am happy to make your acquaintance, as well. I have four sisters already and look forward to adding one more to the mix."

Georgiana's eyes widened. "You have four sisters?" She looked up at her brother and then back at Elizabeth. "I only have one brother. I cannot imagine having four siblings."

Elizabeth winked. "I cannot imagine having a brother. You will have to tell me all about how to tease and torment him."

The girl looked as though she did not know whether to laugh or be horrified. It was Darcy who rescued her.

"You are both quite accomplished at teasing me as it is. I am not so sure I like the idea of you cooperating in such an endeavor." His lips twisted into a smirk, causing his sister to laugh and his betrothed to cover a chuckle with her hand.

Darcy's voice became stern again. "Come, everyone. Do sit down. I have something to convey, and Bingley, it involves you."

Their host's commanding tone made everyone jump, and within seconds, all were seated, Georgiana between Jane and Elizabeth, the Blackwells on a nearby settee, and the earl and countess, as well as the single gentlemen, in the remaining chairs that made up the seating arrangement.

"What has happened?" Lady Matlock barely waited to sit before she asked her question.

In precise language, Darcy explained how his friend's sister had cut Elizabeth. "I will not tolerate anyone causing her distress. It is no fault of hers that an accident I caused resulted in the situation in which we find ourselves." He looked at his friend. "I know you have sanctioned Caroline. You may need to be even stricter with her."

Bingley had become redder the longer Darcy spoke. "I can guarantee you that I will. I apologize to both you and Miss Elizabeth." He turned to Elizabeth. "I am so sorry that my sister behaved in such a heinous manner toward you. Rest assured it will be addressed with her." He paused, pressing his lips together. "I cannot comprehend her motives. We were not raised to be rude to others. I am sorry."

Elizabeth leaned forward a little and looked him in the eye. "Thank you for your apology, but you are not responsible for her behavior. It is Miss Bingley who conducted herself badly and it is she who should bear the consequences. You have been nothing but lovely to us all – to me, especially – since the night of the ball."

Bingley gave her a tight-lipped smile. "Thank you. I promise you, she will be dealt with."

Elizabeth leaned back with a nod. "That is enough for me."

"It is not enough for me, however." Darcy had remained on his feet, watching the interaction between his betrothed and his friend. "I will continue to extend invitations to you, Bingley, but your sister is excluded. Do not bring her here or to any event to which I invite you."

Lady Matlock had quietly listened until that moment, but then had to have her say. "I am in agreement with my nephew." She looked at Bingley. "I have tolerated your sister in my home and at my events out of consideration for your friendship with Darcy. However, Miss Elizabeth will be part of my family and family sticks together." She turned her gaze to her husband, who had audibly gasped. "I know that Lord Matlock has been resistant to the marriage, but the young lady is a gentlewoman who is clearly well-mannered and graceful." She gestured to the sofa on the other side of the room. "Darcy clearly thinks highly of her; he has hardly looked elsewhere, and she has done the same. Not every marriage that is made must be formed with an eye toward political alliances or an increase in wealth. I am not saying they are in love. Not yet, anyway," she added with a sly glance at her nephew. "However, she is of a good family and her father is a gentleman."

Lord Matlock snorted. "No one has ever heard of her father."

"Be that as it may, Uncle," Darcy pointed out. "Mr. Bennet's estate has been in his family for at least two hundred years, as I understand it."

"Indeed." Mrs. Blackwell's countenance had flushed a deep red. A scowl marred her features. "Two hundred and fifty, last I counted." Her chin rose as she glared at the earl.

Lord Matlock harrumphed but said nothing else.

His wife pointed to Annabelle. "There, you see? His estate is not that much newer than yours. The only difference between Mr. Bennet and you is the title you bear."

"And, undoubtedly, the annual income." The earl glowered at his wife for a moment, but when she opened her mouth to speak again, lifted a hand. "I hear what you are saying." He sighed and ground his teeth. "A happy wife results in a happy home, and I much prefer my home to be a pleasant place to live in." He looked at Darcy. "Therefore, it behooves me to accept your lady into the family.

I will add my censure to my wife's and say to you, Bingley, that until your sister apologizes and changes her behavior, she will no longer be welcome in my home."

Darcy's whole body seemed to relax a little. "Thank you, Uncle." He turned to his friend. "I am sorry it has come to this."

Bingley held up a hand. "No, do not feel sorry. I knew it could happen, and I warned her about it. She did not listen, to her detriment. I will take care of it."

"Good." At last, Darcy let down his stance. He perched on the arm of the sofa, next to where Elizabeth was seated. He looked down at his betrothed.

"Well," she said as she met his gaze. "That was momentous." She grinned, and everyone began to laugh.

With the tension now eased, conversation began to flow, with the Matlocks asking questions of the Bennet ladies and the Blackwells, and them replying. Soon, the butler came in to inform Darcy that the meal was ready, and the group filed in pairs into the dining room. As host, Darcy led the way, with Elizabeth on his arm. His aunt and uncle followed. Next came the colonel and Georgiana, and finally, Jane and Bingley.

Chapter 9

The gentlemen settled the ladies into their seats and then took their own. Darcy had not been concerned overmuch about precedence and so had invited his guests to sit where ever they wished. He escorted Elizabeth to sit at his right. He had found over the course of the last week that he greatly enjoyed her conversation and wished to indulge in more of it.

At Darcy's gesture, the servants brought in the first course of the meal and served it before sliding silently away. For a short time, the only sound was that of spoons occasionally striking the rim of a bowl. Soon, though, the initial hunger everyone felt was relieved a bit. Lady Matlock was the first to break her silence, speaking to Elizabeth, who was across the table and down one seat from her.

"Tell me more about yourself, Miss Elizabeth. I understand you are from Hertfordshire?"

Elizabeth rested her spoon on her bowl and turned her attention to the countess. "I am, my lady. My father's estate is called Longbourn. It is near the market town of Meryton."

"Meryton." Lady Matlock looked at her husband, who was seated beside her. "Have we ever stopped there?"

"We have not. I have heard of it, but it is set off the London road quite a bit." He looked at

Elizabeth. "I do not imagine it gets much in the way of traffic."

Elizabeth shook her head. "No, it does not. There is an inn and a post stop, but as you said, it is further from the main road than most people prefer to go when they are travelling between town and the further reaches of the north."

"This is true," the earl conceded. "I would imagine, though, that it makes a direct route to the North Sea and villages along it."

Elizabeth smiled. "It does; many people pass through on their way to Chelmsford or Bradwell-on-Sea. As I understand it, there are some rather fine islands on which one can lease a cottage. I have heard some of the gentlemen in my area speak of the shooting and other sport that can be found there."

"I would imagine one might find some sea-bathing, as well."

Lord Matlock rolled his eyes at his wife's words. "I would imagine so, Audra. No, I am not taking you sea-bathing." He shook his head and applied himself to his second course, which had just been served to him.

Elizabeth bit her lip and looked at her plate, but Lady Matlock did not appear to notice. She was too busy frowning at her husband.

Darcy cleared his throat. "Well, then." He paused and before addressing his betrothed. "Elizabeth, tell us more about your family."

From the other end of the table, Georgiana urged the same. "Oh, do! You told me you have four sisters. Tell us about them."

Elizabeth chuckled, bringing her hand over her mouth to cover it. "Jane, here, is my older sister. As you can see, she is everything lovely." She smiled at her sister, who blushed and thanked her.

"I am the second daughter, and after me comes Mary. She is two years younger than I am and is fond of music. She is very serious in everything, and studious. She is fond of Fordyce's Sermons and dresses quite somberly for a girl of seventeen. She is lovely when you take time to get to know her, but she does not make a particularly good first impression."

"Are you close, then?" Lady Matlock asked while focusing on cutting her meat, though she glanced up at Elizabeth as she did so.

"Not as close as we should be, I suppose. I am closest with Jane; she and I have more in common than I do with Mary."

"Quite understandable." Colonel Fitzwilliam picked up his glass to take a sip. "I have two sisters and an older brother. I am closer to my sister Constance than I am to either my brother or my youngest sister, for the same reason. Though we have different interests now, when we were children, we had more in common." He shrugged. "I suppose that could be because the viscount is so much older and my youngest sister is so much younger and so

Connie and me were together all time, but the fact remains."

"Oh, you and your sister were always getting into some scrape or another." The countess shuddered. "How we managed to keep your governess in our employ I will never know." She turned her attention back to Elizabeth. "You have described two sisters; tell us about the rest."

"Well, the next after Mary is Catherine. We call her Kitty. She is a year younger than Mary and two years older than our youngest sister. Though she is the elder of them, she follows her younger sister in everything. She is a bit silly; I have hope that, as she ages, she will mature." Elizabeth took a sip from her glass. "The youngest is Lydia. She is lively; unabashed and spoiled." She shrugged. "She is our mother's favorite, I think because her personality is so much like Mama's."

"I see." Lady Matlock was quiet for a moment. "What are your youngest sisters' accomplishments?"

Elizabeth looked at Jane, her brows raised, before replying. "Kitty can draw reasonably well, and she has a lovely singing voice. She can sew – we all can – and has excellent needlework skills. She has embroidered many of the doilies that grace our tables. She also enjoys painting."

Jane smiled. "She has a talent for mimicking voices that has been a source of much amusement on a long, cold winter's night."

"That she has!" Elizabeth laughed. "As for Lydia, her skills lie in making over bonnets and such. Her needlework is not as good, and she does not have the patience for drawing or painting or music, though her voice is high and clear and a delight to listen to." She shook her head. "Getting her to practice is a task in and of itself. She dislikes repeating things and simply refuses to do it."

"Perhaps, as with Miss Kitty, these character traits will mature." Darcy watched Elizabeth as she shrugged.

"Perhaps."

Georgiana looked between her brother, Elizabeth, and Jane. "Your sisters sound very interesting. When will we meet them?"

"Oh." Elizabeth faltered, glancing at Darcy and then her aunt and uncle. "Well, I am uncertain when that will be."

"Will they not come for the wedding?" Bingley glanced between his host and Elizabeth.

"I do not believe so. Mr. Bennet should be here, but as I understand it, Mrs. Bennet and the younger Miss Bennets will remain at Longbourn." Darcy leaned back to allow the servant to take his plate.

Lord Matlock looked around at the Blackwells and Bennets. "I suspect an underlying issue here. Are they unsuitable in some way?"

Jane cleared her throat, but it was Annabelle who answered.

"My brother's wife is rather excitable. When overset, she fancies herself ill with nerves. It is better for her to remain calm and at home."

Understanding lit Lady Matlock's face and she explained to her husband, whose creased brow indicated his lack of comprehension. "She is similar to Vanessa's mother." She added, for the benefit of the rest of the party, "Vanessa is our daughter-in-law, the viscountess."

The earl's eyes widened. "Oh, I see." He cleared his throat and looked with sympathy at Darcy and Elizabeth. "Well," he said, "one cannot be held in contempt for the behavior of one's family, can one? I have a difficult sister myself. I can understand your position."

Lady Matlock leaned forward a little. "His sister, whose name is also Catherine." She leaned back and shook her head. "The woman loves to manage everyone else's life."

"That is putting it mildly, Mother." Richard lifted his glass in a salute to her. "Lady Catherine de Bourgh is a harridan."

"Richard! Do not speak of your aunt in such a manner!" Lady Matlock paused. "No matter how true it is."

Everyone laughed and from that point on, the conversation for the rest of the meal turned to more general topics.

~~~***~~~

Two days later, Lord and Lady Matlock hosted a ball. It was something they did every year, and invitations were coveted by all the *ton*. This year, the fact that their nephew was marrying an unknown girl he was caught in a compromising situation with made the invitations even more precious.

Darcy arrived to pick up Elizabeth exactly on time. He was in the entry hall with Blackwell when he heard a noise at the top of the stairs and saw Annabelle, Jane, and Elizabeth about to descend. Though the thought flitted through his mind that they were all handsome, his intense gaze focused on his betrothed; she was the only lady he truly saw.

Elizabeth wore a gown he had never seen before. It was a beautiful shade of purple, a little darker than the lilacs he had in his garden at Pemberley. It was trimmed in white lace, and was accented with a white shawl made of matching white lace that was draped over her arms. The bodice of the dress just hinted at her cleavage and was more modest than most in attendance would be. Her dark hair was swept up into an elaborate coiffure with two or three long curls left hanging over her shoulder. Elbow-length white gloves completed her ensemble. The color became her and her graceful descent combined with her looks and her shy smile left Darcy speechless, his mouth dry.

When she reached the bottom of the stairs,

Elizabeth curtseyed, and Darcy shook himself out of his befuddled state. He bowed. "Good evening, my dear. You are stunning."

Elizabeth blushed and looked down. "Thank you. I am pleased to hear your opinion." She looked up. "Will I fit in with the rest of your aunt's guests, do you think?"

Darcy took her hand and lifted it to her lips, feeling a burn through the gloves they both wore. "Oh, yes. You will be the loveliest woman there and the rest of the attendees will fall at your feet." He chuckled when she smirked at him. "I would like to claim your first set, if I may. I expect my aunt will make this a sort-of engagement ball for us and will demand we dance the first together, anyway, but just in case, I would like to know I have it."

"It is yours." Elizabeth tilted her head as if to see what he would say next.

"May I also request the supper set?"

"You may." She smirked. "Shall I save it for you?"

Darcy chuckled. "Yes, please do."

A throat being cleared drew the couple out of their banter. They had been so immersed in each other that they had failed to notice Bingley's arrival and the rest of the family putting on their wraps. They turned matching shades of red. Darcy took her coat from the maid and helped her into it. They then went out to board Darcy's carriage, which was large enough to easily fit them all.

"Mr. Bingley, were you able to speak to your sister?" Jane asked.

"I was. She reacted much as I expected her to. Badly."

"I am sorry." Jane's voice conveyed the sympathy she felt, though the light in the equipage was too dim for anyone's face to be seen clearly.

"Thank you." Bingley said nothing else, and the rest of the short drive was completed in silence.

When they arrived a scant five minutes later, Darcy was the first to step down from the carriage. He handed Elizabeth out. Blackwell and Bingley followed, each handing out the lady they were escorting. When everyone was together again, Darcy led the way up the shallow set of steps. Before long, they were all inside and greeting Lord and Lady Matlock and their children.

Once past the reception line, Darcy led Elizabeth into the brightly lit, elegant ballroom. With her hand tucked into the crook of his arm, they began to make a circuit around the room, stopping at times to speak to someone Darcy knew. As the space grew increasingly more crowded, the pair stopped near one of the doors where the air was less stifling. They were soon joined by Bingley and Jane.

"I say, this is quite a crush." Bingley looked over his shoulder as another gentleman jostled him while passing by.

"It is." Darcy's countenance was grim. "Far worse than last year, and that was well-attended."

Elizabeth looked up at him. "You do not enjoy these events?"

Darcy shook his head. "I do not." He looked down and shifted his stance before meeting her eyes. "I always feel like a fox being set upon by the hounds." He shrugged when her hand lifted to cover her mouth. "I am known to have a fine fortune and to have been master of my estate at an early age. It is not unheard of for unmarried women and their parents have been known to chase me down at these things." He tipped his head toward his friend. "Ask Bingley if you do not believe me."

Immediately, Elizabeth turned toward the other man, who nodded vigorously.

"It is true. My own sister tried to compromise him last season. He is a very attractive fortune. I mean, gentleman." Bingley grinned when the ladies laughed.

Darcy rolled his eyes. "Thank you. I think."

"Shall we walk around some more?" Elizabeth's eyes shone as she watched all the well-dressed society members wandering past.

Darcy watched his betrothed for a minute and could not deny himself the pleasure of her delight. If it would make her happy, he would walk through Hyde Park in mud to his knees, shoeless. "Of course." He led her into the moving mass of people. He saw out of the corner of his eye that Bingley and Jane stepped out behind them.

They had not gone far when the one person he truly never wished to see again came across their path.

It seemed to Darcy as though the sea had parted and in the middle of the empty space left behind stood Lady Penelope Mays. Elizabeth had seen her, too. He knew because she came to a stop at his side. Darcy glanced down at his betrothed, noted her narrowed eyes and clenched jaw that indicated her feelings matched his, and placed his free hand over the one that rested on his arm. When Elizabeth looked up at him, he lifted his chin. She seemed to catch on, because she did the same. Then, he looked Lady Penelope in the eye and deliberately turned himself and his betrothed away without otherwise acknowledging her. He heard gasps around him when the lady and those near her realized that he and Elizabeth had given her the cut direct.

Chapter 10

Darcy led his betrothed to the other end of the ballroom, Bingley and Jane following close behind. He glanced at Elizabeth, and noted that her jaw remained tight, though she had plastered a pleasant smile on her face. He drew her away to a quiet corner containing some potted plants.

"Bingley, will you and Jane please keep watch over us? I wish to speak to Elizabeth in privacy."

"Of course." Bingley peeked through the branches of the tall ferns. "You cannot do anything untoward back there. It is too easy to be seen. Take as long as you like. Miss Bennet and I will warn you if anyone approaches."

"Thank you." Darcy nodded to his friend and led his betrothed between the pots and into the small space behind them. He moved to face her and took her hands. "Are you well?"

Elizabeth nodded, replying in a whisper to match his. "I am. I can hardly believe I actually cut her like that, but she ruined my reputation when she barely knew me." She paused. "I have tried to forgive her. I have made the choice every single day to do so, but there is clearly still anger in my heart over her actions."

Darcy squeezed her hands. "Mine, as well. I confess I have been holding onto it and not making the choice to forgive." He looked down and bit his lip. "I have a resentful temper, I fear. My good opinion, once lost, is lost forever."

"Well, that is a shade in a character, but one can hardly blame you. I certainly do not." Elizabeth glanced at the foliage beside her and then continued on in the same soft tone. "I have never been so angry with anyone in my entire life. I fear it will take a long time to get over it, despite the relatively pleasant outcome of what she did."

Darcy grinned. "I know what you mean. It is a rather pleasant thing to be betrothed, is it not?" He became serious. "I am sorry she is here. I am a little bit surprised that my aunt and uncle allowed her to enter, but her brother is a viscount and that may have had something to do with it. Uncle may need Westerville's vote on some legislation in Parliament." He looked her directly in the eye. "If she accosts you or creates any kind of trouble for you, I want you to tell me at once. I will make sure she is not received in polite society for a very long time."

Elizabeth nodded. "I hope she does not, but if she does, I will tell you. I do not like the idea of giving tit for tat, but she must have consequences." She sighed. "I am certain my sister Mary would tell me that revenge is wrong, and I do agree, but I cannot help but wish for it."

Darcy smiled at her and freed one hand, lifting it to brush a lock of hair away from her cheek. "I agree." He straightened up and held his elbow out to her again. "Shall we head back into the fray?"

Elizabeth grinned and tucked her hand under his elbow. "We shall."

The couple weaved their way back through the ferns to rejoin Jane and Bingley.

"Well?" Darcy's friend looked from face to face. "Did you say what you needed to?"

"We did." Darcy nodded. "I suppose you noticed our behavior before we spoke?"

Jane glanced at Bingley and then looked at her sister's betrothed. "We did. I did not realize at first who she was, but when I saw her turn red, I knew." Jane blushed. "I feel terrible for this, but Mr. Bingley and I followed your example."

Elizabeth's eyes widened. "You cut her, too?" She pretended to look on either side of Jane. "Who are you, and what have you done to my oh-so-proper, only-sees-the-good-in-people sister?"

Jane rolled her eyes. "Lizzy!" She laughed and shook her head. "You know very well that when someone hurts one of my sisters, they must deal with me."

Elizabeth grinned and squeezed the other girl's arm. "I do. Thank you."

Jane winked but then became somber. "I only hope there are no repercussions for any of us."

Darcy shook his head. "There will not be. I will speak to Westerville and tell him you were following my lead. He is well aware of how his sister is. I will make sure he does not censure you or allow his mother or sister to do it."

"Very well." Bingley glanced at Jane and then looked back at his friend. "I will trust you on this." He paused. "She quite deserved it, and you are not without power in society, despite your lack of a title. I find myself quite tired of self-serving ladies and their machinations."

The rest of the group murmured their agreement. They could not discuss it more because the musicians began to tune up, and Lady Matlock arrived at their sides to urge Darcy and Elizabeth to lead the dancing.

The remainder of the ball passed in a pleasant fashion. Lady Penelope did not approach Elizabeth. In fact, none of the party saw her again after they had cut her. Though the newly engaged couple was looked at askance by many, there were others who either had not heard the gossip, did not believe it, or overlooked it given the betrothal that had resulted. These ladies and gentlemen were the ones who approached Darcy and his bride-to-be with intelligent and pleasing conversation and who made the experience a far better one than the last ball they had attended.

At the end of the night, Darcy dropped Elizabeth and her family off at their house and Bingley at his before finally reaching his own home and his bed. He spent the rest of the night dreaming about Elizabeth's fine eyes and the graceful way she danced.

~~~***~~~

The next day, Darcy arrived at the Blackwell home, Bingley in tow, to find the ladies inundated with callers, both male and female. Though he hated to be on display, he was glad he had come so early, because he was able to give Elizabeth the support of his presence. During a break in visits, he asked how the calls had been.

"Very interesting," Annabelle replied.

Darcy's brows rose. "How so?"

"Well ..." Elizabeth drew the word out. "It seems that all anyone wished to speak of was the cut Lady Penelope received." She paused, lifting her brow. "Apparently, her mother is furious and her brother has sent the female members of his family to their country estate for a long visit."

"I see." Darcy winked at his betrothed. "I am not at all surprised."

"Do not be coy, sir." Elizabeth's lips twitched. "Did you speak to Viscount Westerville?"

"I confess I did. I saw him early this morning when I went riding in the park and confessed to what we had done. He had heard what happened; his mother was furious and made certain he knew of it. I fear things have not gone as she would have wished them to go, however, for he vowed to stop Lady Penelope's bad behavior once and for all. He may have mentioned a long trip to one of his further-flung estates." Darcy laughed when Elizabeth's countenance brightened.

"A fitting punishment, I dare say." Annabelle rose to ring for a fresh tea tray. "Would you like some refreshments, Mr. Darcy? Mr. Bingley?"

"I would not mind a cup of coffee if you have any." Darcy looked toward his friend.

Bingley pulled his attention from Jane. "Tea for me, please."

Mrs. Blackwell nodded to the maid and added instructions for scones and clotted cream to be added to the tray. Then, she dismissed the girl and resumed her seat.

Bingley was addressing the group. "My sister was shocked to hear of you cutting Penelope like you did, Darcy. She could not imagine you behaving so to anyone and was very much regretting that she was unable to witness it." He tipped his head toward Elizabeth. "She blamed it on your betrothed and declared that you would never have done something so awful were you not unduly influenced. I will not repeat the words she used to describe you, Miss Elizabeth."

"Thank you. My imagination is well able to fill in the blanks." Elizabeth's dry tone caused her aunt and sister to giggle.

Bingley grinned. "She was suffering a particularly difficult morning, I confess. She had already been chafing at my refusal to escort

108

her to events in my circle. She has been limited to those of my brother Hurst's for several weeks now. Then when I discovered she had cut you, Miss Elizabeth ... and it just now occurs to me that she called Darcy's behavior rude but does not see that hers was, as well." He shook his head. "Well, when I discovered her behavior towards you, I informed her that I would not pay her overages at the shops and that she is forthwith limited to her pin money. She had a fit that I am certain could be heard on Bond Street. Last evening, I refused to take her to the Matlock ball with me, and explained to her why. She became angry again but was forced to rein herself in or Hurst would refuse to take her along to the soiree had and my sister Louisa were attending. This morning, she is still angry about it all, so her responses to my tale were rather vituperative." He chuckled. "I confess to enjoying her frustration. It is a rare thing for me to gain the upper hand with Caroline. I hope to keep it for a long time."

Darcy smirked. "Or at least until she marries and someone else has to deal with it."

Bingley laughed, as did the ladies. "Indeed," he said.

As the merriment faded, the conversation turned to other topics and before too long, more visitors arrived. The gentlemen stayed with their ladies the rest of the morning, later spending a pleasant hour with Mr. Blackwell and accepting an invitation to dine.

The next day was Sunday, and Darcy again joined his betrothed and her family in their pew at church, followed by a day spent in leisure activities in their home. He had received the special license in the post the day of the ball and had taken the draft of the settlement to his solicitor to have official copies made. Blackwell had told him that Bennet had written back with his plans to arrive in London at the end of the week. While Darcy was surprised at the gentleman's late arrival, given the compromise of his supposedly favorite daughter, he could not control anyone but himself and did his best to let it go.

On Monday, he spent a large portion of the morning attending to his correspondence. Mr. Baxter had presented him with a salver piled high with letters and he now sat at his desk, opening them one by one, scanning the contents, and sorting them into piles.

At the bottom of the stack was a missive that looked odd. The direction had been written in a poor hand, as though a child had addressed it. He did not recognize the handwriting, and the envelope contained no return address. His brow creased as he examined it. Then, with a shrug, he turned it over and broke the paste seal.

> *Mr. Darcy,*
>
> *If you continue with the engagement you have entered into with Miss*

Elizabeth Bennet, you will face consequences you have no way of foreseeing. Your life, your fortune, and your estate are at risk.

The note was unsigned. Darcy stared at it for a long moment, reading the short message a second and then third time. He grimaced at it and rolled his eyes.

"I am not overly concerned," he said to himself. "This is probably a prank, sent by one bored member of society or another." He tossed the message into the grate, where it instantly caught fire and disintegrated. He shook his head as he separated his piles of letters and began to compose responses.

Chapter 11

A few streets away, the residents of the Blackwell home were also receiving their post.

"Lizzy, you and Jane both have letters from home." Blackwell smiled at his nieces and passed the missives along to them. "There is one here for you, my love," he said to his wife.

"Thank you, James." Annabelle caressed her fingers over his as she accepted her letter. She winked at him when he looked up at her, then hid a grin when he winked back.

Blackwell cleared his throat, sent a quick glance to the other side of the table where Elizabeth and Jane sat, and then checked the rest of the mail.

"Oh." His brow creased as he flipped the note in his hand over to examine the back. "Here is another one for you, Lizzy, though I do not recognize the handwriting and there is no indication who sent it."

"How curious." Elizabeth's forehead crinkled as she accepted the note. "I do not recognize it, either. I wonder who it is from." She broke open the seal and unfolded the page.

Miss Elizabeth Bennet,

It would behoove you to end your engagement to Mr. Darcy. The consequences for failing to do so will be swift and severe. If you do not heed this warning, your ruination will be complete. There will be nothing you can do to save your family from shame and the censure of society.

Elizabeth gasped, drawing the attention of her relatives.

"What is the matter, Lizzy?" Jane reached for her sister's hand.

"Do tell us." Blackwell reached to take back the strangely written letter that Elizabeth was still holding.

"I-" Elizabeth shook her head as she handed the missive over to her uncle. "I do not know what to make of it."

Blackwell read it silently, his mien growing grim.

Annabelle touched his arm. "What does it say?"

James' lips flattened, but he read the note aloud, to the gasps of his wife and eldest niece.

Jane squeezed her sister's hand. "Is there no signature?"

Blackwell shook his head. "None." He looked at each of the ladies. "I do not think there is anything to fear, but it would be wise to be cautious. I will assign extra footmen to accompany you when you leave the house. You are not to go anywhere without at least two male servants to guard you. Three if there is more than one of you leaving."

The ladies nodded.

"Good. I will speak to them as soon as I have finished breaking my fast."

"I am sorry that I have caused your household to be disrupted, Uncle."

James touched Elizabeth's arm. "It is no disruption. I would prefer to be prepared for any eventuality, and I often meet with the servants on Mondays, anyway, when our schedule changes or there is something they need to know."

Elizabeth pressed her lips together and nodded. The family applied themselves to completing their meal before separating to their individual activities for the morning.

~~~***~~~

A couple hours later, at a gambling den in another neighborhood, Sir Augustus entered and looked around. He was early; at this time of day, most of the other gamblers he knew were still shaking off the effects of whatever their favorite drink was. He was aware, though, that he might be able to find someone looking for a card player.

There were few members of his class who frequented this particular establishment. Most who came here were lower: wealthy tradesmen, mostly, but also workers who liked their cards but did not wish to play in dens in the worst of the slums and younger sons blessed with allowances large enough that they did not have to rely on their employment to pay their bills. Occasionally, a peer would grace the regulars with his purse, but only now and then.

Sir Augustus accepted a glass of port from the servant who offered it and began to wend his way through the empty tables to one near the back. He could see two full tables of card players and chose to sit at an empty one within earshot and wait for an opening. As he sipped his drink, he listened to the players sitting closest to him.

"What are you doing here, anyway, Wickham? I thought you had a living up in Derbyshire."

The man addressed as Wickham snorted as he picked up the cards dealt to him. "Darcy refuses to give it to me. Tells me I signed my rights to it away."

Sir Augustus leaned closer in an effort to hear better as another player spoke.

"Do you not have legal recourse?"

"Who can afford representation? I certainly cannot." Wickham shook his head. "My godfather must be rolling in his grave over this. I was his favorite and Darcy knows it. He is jealous and this is his revenge." He plucked a coin from the stack in front of him and tossed it into the pile in the center of the table. "However, I have a plan to get my own back and more."

Sir Augustus listened with one ear to the rest of the conversation. *The gentleman clearly has it out for Darcy,* he thought. *Perhaps I can use him to get that interfering sot out of the way so I can claim Elizabeth for myself.*

Though he had to wait for nearly an hour, eventually the play at the other table broke up and Sir Augustus was able to approach Wickham, who remained sitting as he counted his winnings.

"Might I buy you a drink?"

Wickham looked up, brows raised. He examined Augustus closely and shrugged before turning his attention back to the pile of coins in front of him. "If you like." He pulled a purse out of his pocket and began to fill it.

The baron gestured to a footman, who brought over two glasses and placed them on the table.

"I heard you mention Darcy. Did you mean Mr. Darcy of Pemberley? Do you know him well?" Sir Augustus kept his eyes on Wickham, assessing his demeanor and behavior.

"I do. Why?"

The baron shrugged. "I am also acquainted with him. It sounded as though he behaved rather infamously with you."

The other man's gaze narrowed as he took his time answering. Finally, he said, "He did. What is it to you?"

"He has done the same to me. If you are

half as angry as I am, you would do nearly anything to extract vengeance."

"I would." Wickham lifted his chin. "If you were listening in on my conversation, as it appears you must have, you know that I have a plan to extract more from him than just his money."

"Mmmhm." The baron took a sip of his port. "Indeed." He paused and then looked Wickham in the eye. "I can probably help you with that." He held up a hand. "I do not know exactly what revenge you plan, but if you assist me in separating him from a lady, I will help you execute your retaliation."

"Who are you?" Wickham turned in his chair to face the man who sat beside him.

"I am Baron Whitestone, Sir Augustus Perry."

Wickham's brows shot up as his eyes widened. He extended his hand. "George Wickham."

The men shook hands.

Wickham leaned back. "Darcy has stolen your lady from you? Hard to imagine that stick in the mud knowing what to do with a woman."

Sir Augustus flushed. "He did, but with your help, she will soon be begging me to renew my offer to her."

"What is it you wish me to do? I will not commit until I have details."

The baron narrowed his eyes but nodded. "Very wise." He leaned forward and lowered his voice. "I have heard for years that Darcy's aunt in Kent, Lady Catherine de Bourgh, claims an engagement between him and her daughter. I want you to go to her estate and persuade her to come to London and force him to end his betrothal to Elizabeth Bennet."

Wickham picked up the cards and began shuffling them. "I see. What is in it for me?"

Perry sat back. "I will pay your expenses and write a letter to the lady for you to deliver. Once the deed is done and Darcy has walked away from Elizabeth, I will assist you in implementing your plans."

"Hm." Wickham eyed the baron up and down as he considered his options. "I want more than just my expenses paid. I have interacted with Lady Catherine in the past; she is a difficult woman to deal with. I want compensation for putting up with her."

Perry stiffened, scowling. "Very well. I will pay you five hundred pounds, half up front and half after I marry Elizabeth."

After a few more minutes of contemplation, Wickham dropped the cards he had been playing with and held out his hand. "You have a deal. When do you want me to go to Rosings?"

The pair then hammered out the rest of the details. Sir Augustus handed over the funds he had on his person and gave his new henchman instructions on when and where to pick up the rest of the two hundred fifty pound down payment. Wickham agreed to meet him at the specified time, and they walked out of the club together.

~~~***~~~

The next day, in the middle of the morning, George Wickham got off the post coach in the town closest to Rosings. He walked the short distance from the village to the estate, whistling all the way. He had spent hours considering how to approach Darcy's aunt. He was certain he could persuade her to leave with him, though he knew she was immune to his charm.

Soon, he approached the house with its rows of windows. Shaking his head, he thought about the wealth represented. "Well," he muttered under his breath, "if my plans for Darcy's sister go as I intend, I will also live like a king, for a very long time."

He took the shallow steps two at a time and rang the bell. Within moments, the butler had answered the door and escorted him inside.

"Wait here while I see if the mistress is available."

Wickham nodded and examined the furnishings until the servant returned.

"Lady Catherine will see you now."

When he entered the large drawing room, the lady of the house stood. He bowed to her. "Good day, my lady. It has been a long time since I have seen you."

Lady Catherine looked him up and down, her mien registering her disapproval. "My butler said you had news of Darcy."

Wickham smiled. "Indeed, I do. He has be-
120

trothed himself to some girl or other." He reached into his pocket and pulled out the letter Perry had written. "Baron Whitestone has tasked me with bringing you the news. He wished me to present this missive to you."

Her lips pressed together, the mistress of Rosings accepted the note. She resumed her seat, though she did not invite her visitor to sit down. She examined the seal that closed the letter, then broke it open, unfolded it, and read it in silence. Her only reaction was a narrowing of her eyes and a twitch in her jaw. She read the entire missive a second time, then stared at it for a few minutes. Wickham could see that she was deep in thought. He shifted on his feet. Eventually, his patience was rewarded.

"I will call for my coach. We should be able to reach London before dark if we leave immediately." Lady Catherine looked him up and down again. "I assume you rode post to get here."

"I did." Wickham gave her his most charming smile and laughed to himself to see her lips twist in disgust.

"You might as well ride with me. My coachman will appreciate the company, I am sure, and your presence will mean I do not have to take one of my grooms along. You can open and close the door."

A half-smile lifted the corners of Wickham's lips. He could not prevent the roll of his eyes at her comments, but Lady Catherine had reached for the bell pull and did not notice. He was grateful to be spared her reaction.

The staff in the stables at Rosings was well-trained and used to bending to the whims of their mistress. Within a half-hour, Lady Catherine was on her way to town, rehearsing her arguments to Darcy.

Chapter 12

Madeline Gardiner greeted her nieces with open arms. She kissed Jane's cheek and hugged her, then took Elizabeth's hands.

"How are you, my dear?"

Elizabeth kissed Maddie's cheek. "I am well." When her aunt's look turned skeptical, she squeezed her hands. "I am. I promise. I am finding more to like about Mr. Darcy every time I see him."

"I am glad. I expected to see him arrive with you." Maddie hugged her younger niece and then greeted the Blackwells.

"He was delayed and took his own carriage," Elizabeth replied as one aunt hugged the other. "He assured us he would arrive shortly after we did."

"Well, then," Maddie said with a grin, "let us repair to the drawing room. Only a few of the guests are here as of yet."

Elizabeth, Jane, and their Blackwell relatives followed Maddie into the comfortable and well-appointed room. Most of the guests were already acquainted with the Bennet girls, so the majority of the introductions involved Annabelle and James. The four entered easily into conversation with the barristers, solicitors, clergymen, and business owners and their wives who made up the group.

Finally, Darcy and Bingley also arrived and were introduced. By then, the remainder of those invited were in the house, and so the party proceeded into the dining room.

The evening went very well, in Elizabeth's opinion. No one cut her and she was not required to do the same to anyone else. After the meal, she and Darcy were paired at the vingt-et-un table with the Gardiners, and then played lottery tickets with the Blackwells. They paired up again for whist with another couple: a newly married barrister and his young wife.

Elizabeth's uncle approached her and her betrothed in a break between games. "Are you enjoying yourselves?"

"I am." Elizabeth grinned at Mr. Gardiner and turned to Darcy to listen to his reply.

"I am, as well. Your guests are friendly and engaging. The conversation tonight has been excellent." Darcy smiled down at Elizabeth. "I enjoy watching my betrothed try to hide her excitement when she wins."

Elizabeth laughed, her countenance reddening. "Clearly I must try harder to mask it."

"No, no. It is charming." Darcy moved closer to her.

"Well, thank you." She turned to her uncle, who was looking between them with a growing grin. "Thank you for inviting us."

Gardiner shrugged. "Your aunt has been after me for weeks to have some sort of party while you were still in town. Once you were ..." He paused as though looking for the word he wanted. "Engaged, we wished to show our support." He tipped his head toward the other guests. "Some of these people are avid readers of the society pages and came to us with questions. I felt it was imperative that we stand behind you."

Elizabeth put her hand on his arm. "I thank you. Your love never wavers, and that means so much to me."

Darcy reached to shake Gardiner's hand. "I thank you, as well. I know we are from different circles, but gossip does not stay within class lines. I appreciate your assistance in clearing our names."

"I could do no less. If there is any way Maddie and I can help smooth your path, you need only ask."

Gardiner was called away at that moment. Darcy and Elizabeth joined Jane and Bingley to play Commerce, and the remainder of the evening passed just as pleasantly as the beginning had.

~~~***~~~

The next morning, Darcy was up early to ride in Hyde Park, as was his wont. He returned the mare to the stables in the mews behind Darcy House, and after speaking to

125

the stable master for a few minutes, strode across the way to the back garden of his home. A cry caught his attention and he stopped, cocking his head to listen.

All was silent for a few heartbeats. He was just about to start walking again when he heard the faint cry once more. He turned and made his way toward the sound.

Darcy House took up the entire space between two side streets. It fronted Brook Street and stretched between James and Bird Streets. The sound emanated from the direction of James Street, and so that is where he headed. At the corner was a tall hedge that bordered his property. Unfortunately for Darcy, the hedge was quite thick, and capable of hiding more than just a kitten or child.

He began to search the bushes for the source of the noise, his entire focus on locating whoever or whatever it was. Suddenly, he found himself pitching forward, pain exploding in his back. He was hauled up, and before he could get his bearings, was struck in the face. He staggered backwards and was pushed forward again. Though he attempted to defend himself, he was kept off-balance by multiple assailants raining blows to his face and body. All thought ceased as his focus narrowed to surviving the ordeal. Soon, his strength began to flag. He had just taken a particularly vicious blow to the kidneys when he heard a yell from far away. The incoming fists stopped and he collapsed.

"Darcy! Darcy! Speak to me."

Darcy moaned at the sound of Bingley's voice. He could hear running feet and someone else shouting orders.

"I am here, Darcy, and so is the colonel. Stay with me. The servants are going to take you into the house. It may hurt; prepare yourself."

"How is he?" Richard swore. "Darcy, you must awaken and tell me what happened. Be careful with him boys, he has taken a terrible beating. There may be internal damage."

Darcy knew he should speak, but he could not summon the energy to do so. He felt the footmen lift him up and get him on his feet. He groaned as they stretched his arms over their shoulders and half-dragged, half-carried him into the house.

A short time later, Darcy was on his bed with his valet and housekeeper attending to him. His cousin and friend were in the room, as well, and he could hear Richard badgering the housekeeper about calling the doctor.

"He is on his way, sir. In the meantime, I have sent for ice to be chipped out of the block in the ice box and Smith is preparing to wash him." Mrs. Bishop was firm but respectful.

Darcy needed to turn his cousin's attention to himself and away from the housekeeper, so he called out to the other man. "Fitzwilliam." He was dismayed to realize that his voice was no more than a whisper. He began to gather his strength to try again, when his friend stopped him.

"Darcy?" Bingley rushed to the side of the bed. "Are you awake?"

Darcy tried to lick his lips. "I am."

"He is awake!" Bingley's cry brought Fitzwilliam and Mrs. Bishop to his side, as well.

"It is about time, Cousin." Darcy felt Fitzwilliam's strong grip on his hand. "Can you tell me who did this to you?"

Darcy shook his head slowly from side to side. "No," he whispered.

"Can you tell us how many there were?"

Another shake. "No. At least two."

"Two is all I saw." Bingley's voice this time.

"Perhaps we have them all, then." Richard paused. "I met up with Bingley on my way to your house. Providential, that. When we rounded the corner, we could hear the commotion. I was horrified to find you fighting for your life."

"The colonel here was quite a sight to see, Darcy. I was more startled by his whoop than the sight of you, to be honest. Fitzwilliam pulled out his sword and leaped off his horse and had waded into the fray before I could even figure out what was going on."

Darcy chuckled, then winced at the pain in his side. "How bad is it?"

"Well, your face is not as pretty as it used to

be. The doctor will be here soon to examine you. We will know then if you have broken anything or suffered other injuries." The colonel paused. "Here is the ice. Mrs. Bishop is going to apply it to your eyes first, I would imagine."

"Good," Darcy whispered. "I would prefer looking at you through more than slits when I speak to you."

~~~***~~~

That evening, Darcy remained in his rooms. Bingley and Fitzwilliam stayed with him.

The physician had come, tapped his ribs and examined his limbs and hands, and had declared him as healthy as possible for one who had suffered a beating. He had administered a bit of laudanum to ease the pain and left instructions for poultices to be made and applied to the bruising on Darcy's chest and back. Smith had then assisted his master in washing up.

Once tucked into bed, Darcy held ice to his eyes and mouth until Fitzwilliam insisted a raw steak would do a much better job of relieving the bruising and swelling. Three trays had been brought up containing a hearty luncheon, and the two uninjured gentlemen were now enjoying a repast of a hearty stew and a fresh loaf of bread. Darcy was sipping soup, the swelling in his face having gone down enough that he could open his eyes a bit further, though not enough that he could do more than sip liquids.

"The magistrate was here while you were with the doctor." Fitzwilliam leaned back in his chair and lifted his glass to take a sip. "The two miscreants who beat you will not give up the name of their employer, but they did admit they were hired to attack you."

"Who would want to harm Darcy like that?" Bingley shook his head. "He does not gamble, at least as far as I know, and does not dally with women."

Darcy paused, his spoon part of the way to his mouth. The memory of the letter he had received the day before flashed into his mind. He slowly lifted the spoon, tipped the contents into the space between his bruised lips, and set the utensil down again.

"What is it, Darcy?" Colonel Fitzwilliam's voice was sharp. "What are you thinking about?"

"I got a note yesterday. Unsigned. It had a threatening tone to it."

Richard sat forward, a crease forming between his brows. "Where is this note?"

Darcy shook his head. "I threw it in the fire. I considered it a prank. Now, I wonder."

Richard pressed his lips together as he sat back. "That was a stupid move, Cousin, but there is nothing to be done about it now. If you get any more, show them to me."

"I will. Speaking of letters, I wanted to send

a message to Elizabeth but have been prevented at every turn. I must do so now."

Bingley held up a hand. "Never fear! I sent a servant to Bruton Street as soon as we got in the house, and followed up with a note for Blackwell the moment we knew your condition. They are aware of what happened. I would not be surprised if the man did not drop by this evening to check on you."

Relief coursed through Darcy's being and he closed his eyes. "Thank you. I feel better knowing Elizabeth is not wondering ..." He trailed off.

"Whether you have changed your mind?" The colonel smiled softly.

"I would never do that. Not to her." Darcy opened his eyes to look at his friends. "I wish I could see her and assure her myself that I am well."

"No." Bingley laughed. "You do not. She would be frightened out of her wits to see you as you are at this moment."

"That bad, is it?" Darcy frowned, or tried to.

Fitzwilliam stood and walked into the dressing room, coming back a few minutes later with a small looking glass in his hand. "Here," he said. "Take a look for yourself."

Darcy accepted the glass, glancing up at his cousin. He held it up to his face and cringed at the black and purple bruises that colored his jaw and cheeks, and the black rings around his eyes. He handed the glass back. "Where is that steak?"

Richard and Bingley laughed.

"You will have to stay in for a few days, at least. Perhaps once the colors have faded, Blackwell can bring Miss Elizabeth over here." Bingley chuckled at his friend's creased brow and downcast look.

"I suppose I will." He brightened as a thought entered his mind. "Perhaps we can write to each other. It is not the same as a visit, but it is an acceptable substitute."

The colonel laughed heartily. "Oh, you are besotted, are you not?"

Someone knocked on the dressing room door, catching the gentlemen's attention. Smith appeared in the doorway with a note in his hand.

"Colonel, this has just come from Matlock House."

Fitzwilliam's brows drew together as he accepted the missive. "I wonder what this could be about." He broke the seal, unfolded the page, and read silently. Suddenly, he jumped to his feet. "Oh my word!" His eyes rapidly travelled the rest of the letter, then returned to the top to read it again.

"What has happened?" Darcy sat up straighter in the bed. "Fitzwilliam!"

The colonel lowered the paper. "Our aunt, Lady Catherine de Bourgh, has died in a carriage accident."

Darcy gasped. "What? How? When? What was she doing travelling in January? She never leaves Rosings at this time of year."

"I do not know. Father did not include details, except for this: George Wickham was also involved. He was apparently sitting up beside the driver." Richard paused. "There were no survivors."

Darcy shrank back against the pillows, stunned. "What was George Wickham doing riding on my aunt's carriage? I cannot fathom it. She has always said he was grasping and too charming by half. What could have possibly come about that led to them being in an equipage together?"

Fitzwilliam shook his head. "I do not know, but Father wishes for me to attend him." He paused. "This may delay your wedding."

Darcy shook his head. "No, I have a special license, and we planned on marrying quietly in the Blackwells' front parlor. We can move the ceremony over here. There will be no more balls or outings, but there would not be, anyway, with my injuries."

Richard nodded. "Very well." He tucked the note into his pocket and bowed. "I will leave you now. Get some rest. I hope to bring you the entire story when I come back."

Chapter 13

The next day, Richard returned as promised. Darcy was out of bed, dressed, and in his study. The swelling in his face had gone down significantly, but the bruising had, if anything, gotten worse.

"Colonel Fitzwilliam, sir." Baxter bowed and allowed Richard to move past him, then silently exited the room, pulling the door closed.

Darcy braced himself on the desk with his bruised hands and began to rise. His muscles had stiffened as he sat in the chair, and the contusions on his torso combined with them to make him ache.

"No, no. Sit down. You do not need to stand for me." Fitzwilliam examined his cousin carefully. "You have taken nothing for the pain?"

Darcy sighed in relief once his bottom was resting on the seat of the chair. "No, I have not. I can bear it without drugs." He chuckled and lifted a missive off the desk. "Elizabeth has written to tell me to send someone to the apothecary for willow bark. She says that, made into a tea, it is quite effective at relieving pain. I have asked Mrs. Bishop to see to it."

At that moment, the housekeeper's voice was heard in the hall, followed by a knock on the door.

"Come." Darcy grimaced at the feeling that accompanied the effort of raising his voice.

Mrs. Bishop sailed into the room holding a teacup. "Here you are sir, just as Miss Elizabeth ordered. You take all of this, now. It does not taste any better than laudanum, if you ask me, but your young lady assured me of its efficacy."

Darcy lifted the corners of his lips. "Thank you." He tilted his head to look up at her. "Miss Elizabeth assured you?"

The housekeeper blushed. "Yes, sir. She was with her uncle when he delivered your note this morning and asked to speak to me. She only had a few minutes, as she and her family were on their way to Bond Street, but she wished to make sure I knew how to prepare the concoction."

Darcy shook his head and tried to suppress a laugh. "I see. Thank you, and if she comes back, thank her for me."

"I will, sir." She curtseyed. "Hopefully, you will be able to tell her yourself." With that, she dipped a second curtsey, this time to the colonel, and quietly made her way into the hall.

Fitzwilliam laughed. "You two are going to get on very well together, I daresay. It seems she cares for you as much as you do for her."

A soft smile lit Darcy's bruised features as he lifted the cup to his mouth. He sipped the tea, made a face, and then drained the cup, shuddering as he set it down on its saucer.

"Nasty stuff?"

"Heavens, yes." Darcy shuddered again. He relaxed into his chair, determined to ignore the leftover flavor in his mouth. "What have you discovered?" He gestured to the black band on his cousin's arm.

The colonel sat back and crossed his legs. "Father sent someone to Rosings to find out what he could, and the man returned about an hour ago. Our aunt's butler informed him that Wickham showed up yesterday in the late morning and asked to see Lady Catherine. He was there perhaps a quarter hour when Aunt Cathy summoned her barouche box for a trip to London. She left behind a groom because, she said, Wickham could serve the office and she was neither paying his way back to town nor allowing him to ride inside with her."

Darcy's brows rose. "I wonder what he said to her to convince her to hie off to town on a moment's notice?"

The colonel shook his head. "No one knows at this point. Father sent his man back to Kent to see what else he can discover."

"What about the accident?"

"It seems they had not long left Bromley behind and the coachman had the horses whipped up."

"Likely at Lady Catherine's insistence," Darcy murmured.

"Most likely." Richard's head nodded in agreement. "At any rate, witnesses have related that they were travelling at a high rate of speed when one of the wheels hit a hole in the road and broke. The force of wheel breaking made the barouche swing wildly, startling the horses. Eventually, the carriage rolled over. Wickham and the coachman hit the ground head first. They likely died instantly. Lady Catherine lingered for a little while but was gone by the time the physician arrived at the scene."

Darcy closed his eyes and sighed deeply. "I am saddened at her passing. She liked to meddle too much in my affairs, but she was my mother's sister." He looked at Richard. "What of Anne?"

"Mother should have arrived by now, and Father intends to follow."

"She will inherit."

Richard tilted his head as he tried to read Darcy's expression. "Are you wishing you were not engaged to Miss Elizabeth but were available to offer for our cousin?"

Darcy's eyes popped open. "Good Lord, no! Are you out of your mind?"

The colonel laughed. "Just checking. Anne has told me many times that she did not want to be your wife. I would be surprised if she married at all at this point."

"You could marry her. She likes you better than me and always has."

Richard shrugged. "I doubt she would want a soldier."

Darcy snorted. "You would not remain a soldier if you wed her. She is an heiress, after all."

Richard said nothing, instead changing the subject. "How do you feel about Wickham?"

Darcy was quiet a long time. "I feel ... regretful, I suppose. I regret the friendship we should have had. I regret that my father's favorite turned out as badly as he did and used him like he did. I am relieved he is gone. He will never bother me again. I can relax my vigilance where he is concerned."

"He was not a good man." Fitzwilliam looked down.

"No." Darcy's head shook. "He was not. He was given lessons by his mother that no amount of training could replace. She was always urging him to ingratiate himself with my father, even from a young age. I can remember hearing her urge him to perform, as it were, for Papa. He was spoiled as an only child and taught that he deserved what I had." He shrugged. "Given his propensities as an adult, I find his end to be fitting. It is sad that it must be so, but there it is."

Fitzwilliam nodded. "I agree. Ultimately, the source of his behavior was his own choices, but he certainly was encouraged to think wrongly as a child. Upbringing is difficult to overcome."

The pair fell silent as they thought about the wasted life of their former friend.

~~~***~~~

The following day, Darcy received a note from Blackwell that Mr. Bennet had arrived. Though the missive invited him to attend them at Bruton Street, Darcy's injuries were such that he did not feel up to going out. Instead, he replied with an invitation for the Bennets and Blackwells to come to Brook Street, instead. An acceptance was soon received, and Darcy rang for Mrs. Bishop to prepare for five dinner guests.

"I am sorry for making the request with such short notice. Please assure Cook that whatever she has on hand will be fine."

"Yes, sir." The housekeeper curtseyed and hurried off to do his bidding.

Later that afternoon, Darcy stood in the entry hall as Elizabeth came in behind her aunt and uncle and on her father's arm. He bowed, covering a grimace as best he could.

"Welcome. I am happy you could come." He waited while the maids relieved the group of their outerwear.

"Thank you for inviting us." Blackwell winced to see the colorful patches on his host's face. "You look like the devil. To what extent were you injured?"

Darcy snorted. "I feel like the devil. I am mostly just bruised. The physician found no evidence of broken ribs or anything internal. I will heal within a few days, I daresay." He paused, looking toward Mr. Bennet. "Will you introduce me to your guest?"

"Of course." Blackwell turned and gestured Bennet forward. "This is Annabelle's brother, Mr. Thomas Bennet of Longbourn in Hertfordshire. Thomas, this is Lizzy's betrothed, Mr. Fitzwilliam Darcy of Pemberley in Derbyshire."

The gentlemen bowed to each other.

Bennet examined his future son-in-law carefully. "I am pleased to make your acquaintance, sir."

"I am happy to meet you, as well." Darcy gestured down the hall. "Will you all not come in and sit? I have ordered dinner to be served in an hour or so." He allowed the group to pass, holding his elbow out for Elizabeth to take.

"You do not look too terrible," she whispered to him. "How do you feel?"

"Like I have gone a dozen rounds at Gentleman Jack's," he replied softly. "I ache, but the tea you suggested has relieved much of the pain."

"Good." Elizabeth smiled up at him and squeezed his arm. "You do not look as bad as I had feared from Mr. Bingley's note. You must tell us all what happened."

Darcy smiled at her as best he could. At that point, they had entered the drawing room.

"Please be seated." He assisted Elizabeth to a settee and, after his guests were comfortably situated, sat beside her. He then explained to the assembled group what had happened two days earlier.

"You poor dear!" Annabelle's hand was pressed to her heart. "No wonder you look as you do!"

"Do you know who did this?" Bennet's brow was creased. "I have only just now met you, but if you are the upstanding young man my brother insists you are, I can see no earthly reason for this to have happened."

"My cousin detained the actors, who have admitted they were paid to do it but not who it was who hired them." He shrugged. "The magistrate has them now. I would imagine they are in Newgate at this point. Without knowing who set them to it, I have no idea who was responsible. I can think of no one I have offended to the point of violence."

Blackwell and Bennet looked at each other. Elizabeth bit her lip.

"I confess to being worried for my niece's safety." Blackwell gestured toward Elizabeth. "She received a letter a couple days ago in the post. It was anonymous ... unsigned ... and it was threatening. I have assigned extra footmen to be with my wife and both my nieces any time they leave the house, but your attack increases my unease."

Darcy had startled when he heard this news. "I also got a missive recently, identical to what you described. I did not take it seriously and burned it." He paused and looked to the floor for a moment. "My cousin thinks that an error and after hearing that my betrothed also got one, I am inclined to agree." He looked up. "If you require more servants to guard the ladies, I am happy to provide some to you."

Blackwell nodded. "Thank you for the offer. We are adequately staffed for the moment, but I will be sure to come to you should that change."

Darcy tipped his head in acquiescence and then turned to Bennet. "I am certain you have questions for me, sir. Are there any I can answer now, or would you rather wait until after we eat?"

"I do have questions for you, though your explanation of what happened to you answers some of them." Bennet nodded toward Elizabeth. "My daughter and brother relayed the entirety of the situation that led to your engagement. That was a spectacular step to take, betrothing yourself to a stranger. What could be the reason?" He waved his hand toward his future son. "You could have walked away with few consequences. Certainly, with no lasting ones. What possessed you to attach yourself to my Lizzy?"

Darcy paused before answering. His reason now was the same in essentials as it had been more than a fortnight ago when the event happened, but now that he knew Elizabeth better and recognized his burgeoning feelings for her, it was, at the same time, different. "My first response was to retain my honor and that of my family name. I could see, though, from Miss Elizabeth's expressions and actions that she had not set out to trap me. She was as much an innocent victim in the affair as I was, a fact that was borne out in the recitation of how she came to be in the gentlemen's retiring room.

"That was only at first, though. Now I may add that, as I have come to know her, I have learned that she is everything lovely. She is well-mannered, accomplished, and so very similar to me in every way. I cannot now imagine myself wed to anyone else." He looked to his side to see the blushing, smiling face of that very woman. If he was not mistaken, there was admiration in her eyes, as well, and his heart beat faster to see it.

"That was a very pretty answer, sir." Bennet chuckled, his eyes on his daughter. "I can see that Lizzy thinks the same thing. All I can do is to thank you for your actions. You may have saved your honor and your family name, but you also saved my daughter's reputation. That is not a small thing."

Darcy's eyes had moved to gaze again at Elizabeth, and her blush and shy smile charmed him. He reached for her hand and, lifting it to his mouth, said, "I could do no less." Then, he pressed his lips to her fingers, allowing them to linger as he stared into her eyes.

Chapter 14

Late the next morning, Darcy was in his study with his correspondence in his hand. He was sorting the letters into piles in preparation for reading and replying to them or tossing them in the fire. He had the door open, a sign to his staff that they could freely interrupt him as needed. He got to the last missive in the stack just as the butler rapped on the door frame.

"Sir, Mr. Drover has asked to speak to you."

"Bring him in." Darcy placed the final note in the appropriate pile and straightened each stack, lining them up across the top of the desk away from him. He looked up again when the coachman entered.

"Thank you for seeing me, sir." Drover bowed.

Darcy nodded. "What can I do for you?"

Mr. Drover was clearly trying not to stare at his master's face. "Two of the wheels on the smaller carriage are in need of repairs that I and my staff cannot perform. I would like permission to take them to the wheelwright and see what he can do. They may need to be replaced, of course, but I rather hope they can be repaired."

Darcy thought for a brief moment but then nodded. "You may take them. Do not hesitate to have them replaced, if necessary. I would rather spend money on items that will keep me and my sister safe than to not do so and someone get injured as a result." He unlocked the bottom drawer of his desk, pulled out a small purse, and extracted some funds, which he laid on top of the blotter. Then, he stowed the purse away again and relocked the receptacle before counting the money and handing it to Mr. Drover. "If that is not enough, let me know and I will supplement it."

The coachman accepted the bills, folding them and tucking them into the pocket of his coat. "Thank you, sir. I will do that." He hesitated, biting his lip for a moment, before blurting out a question. "Does it hurt much?"

Darcy's brows rose and dropped. His hand lifted to gently touch his jaw. "Not too much, as long as I do not lay on it or try to scratch it. Mrs. Bishop keeps me well supplied with willow bark tea and that keeps much of the discomfort away." He stood and held out his hand. "I owe you and the boys a debt for responding so quickly to my cousin's orders. He told me you were already on your way to aid me when he and Bingley arrived. Thank you for your care."

Drover shook Darcy's hand. "It was nothing, sir. You would have done the same for any of us, I am certain. You are a good master. I would not want to work for anyone else." He bowed. "I will be on my way. Thank you again, Mr. Darcy."

Darcy inclined his head and watched the

servant leave. Then, with a sigh, he turned back to his correspondence.

~~~***~~~

Sir Augustus paced his sitting room, a newssheet in his hand, muttering invectives about those he hired to work for him. He stopped and read the notice again.

> *We are saddened to announce the passing of Lady Catherine de Bourgh of Rosings, Kent, of injuries sustained in a carriage accident this past Tuesday. Lady Catherine was preceded in death by her husband of twenty years, Sir Lewis de Bourgh. She leaves behind a daughter, Miss Anne de Bourgh, a brother, the Earl of Matlock, Lord Henry Fitzwilliam and his wife, nephews the Viscount Tansley, Lord Trevor Fitzwilliam and his wife, Colonel Richard Fitzwilliam, and Mr. Fitzwilliam Darcy of Pemberley, as well as nieces Lady Constance Fitzwilliam, Lady Susan Fitzwilliam, and Miss Georgiana Darcy.*

Further down the page, there was a smaller notice for a George Wickham, and Perry wondered who had put it there. Wickham had not seemed to him to be someone with a family who would do such a thing. He shrugged and rolled his eyes.

The baron was frustrated. His impromptu

147

plan of bringing Lady Catherine to break up Darcy and Elizabeth's betrothal was clearly impossible now. He had sent some of his most trusted servants to Darcy House to discover what had come about as a result of the beating he had paid to have done only to find that the thugs he had hired had been caught red-handed by Darcy's cousin and were now in prison awaiting trial. What he had intended to be life-threatening to his rival had instead been merely inconvenient.

Resuming his path across the room, the baron spoke out loud, knowing no one would hear him.

"All is well. I have more irons in the fire. Elizabeth will be mine one way or another."

With those words, he threw the newspaper into the fire before marching out of the sitting room and down the stairs.

~~~***~~~

Darcy signed the last of his replies to the morning's post with a flourish. The beating he had taken had led to headaches, and his brain was currently drumming out a pounding rhythm in his skull. He was eager to retire to his rooms for an hour or two of rest. The sound of feet hurrying toward his study made him pause.

"Mr. Darcy." The butler gasped for breath, his countenance florid. "Sir, we have received word from Drover of an accident."

Darcy stood and came around his desk. "An accident? What do you mean? Did one of the wheels break before he could get to the shop?"

Baxter's head shook. He swallowed before he replied, his breathing beginning to calm. "No, sir, not exactly. He told the messenger to tell us that the wheel fell off and that it appeared the axle broke."

Darcy's brows drew together. "He sent a messenger? Did he say if he was well?"

With a nod, the butler replied. "He said he was fine, just a bit shook up. I would imagine he was going slowly enough that he did not get thrown off or anything."

Darcy nodded, his frown still in place. "Good. This is just the sort of thing we were hoping to avoid." He straightened. "Send one of the boys to Drover with two horses to bring him back. Robbie will do; he is an excellent rider. He can ride one animal and lead the other. If he finds John with an injury that will not allow him to ride, he can hire a hack for him. Make sure to give Robbie the funds for it. Tell him to have the carriage towed to the wheelwright as planned. If it needs to go to the carriage maker after that, we will deal with it then. Also, if when John comes back he is injured, have the apothecary notified. It might not hurt to send a note around to him now so he is prepared."

"Very good, sir. I will take care of it immediately." Baxter bowed, his breathing now evened out and his color starting to fade to a more normal one. He turned on his heel and made haste down the stairs to his office.

Darcy turned, his mind full of the fact that his carriage axle had broken. Though he was not one to imagine dramatics where there was none, in light of the threatening letter and the beating he had received, he could not help but wonder if the axle had, in fact, been tampered with. *I suppose I will find out soon enough,* he thought. He sat down at his desk to write one more missive, then rang the bell to have a messenger take it to his cousin.

~~~***~~~

Evening finally arrived at Darcy House and with it, the Bennets and Blackwells for another evening together. Shortly after they arrived, Colonel Fitzwilliam and Bingley were announced, having reached the house at the same time but from different directions.

Once greetings were exchanged, introductions to Mr. Bennet made to the colonel and Bingley, and seats taken, conversation began.

"Has anything untoward happened today?" Bennet smirked. "Anyone jump out of the closet at you?"

Darcy grimaced. "Actually, something did, though not to me, personally. My carriage axle broke this morning. Thankfully, I was not with it."

Gasps broke out around the room.

"I sent my cousin to the wheelwright's shop to find out what he could." He turned to the colonel. "I am eager to hear what he has discovered."

Fitzwilliam's mien was as sober as anyone in the room had ever seen. "I examined the axle and spoke to the wright. It had been cut. It was nearly in two pieces when your coachman set out and it was a miracle it did not break earlier in his journey."

"It was tampered with, then." Blackwell shook his head. "Someone is clearly out to get you, Darcy."

"So it seems," Darcy replied unhappily. "I just cannot imagine who."

Elizabeth, who was seated beside him, laid her hand on his arm. "You must be more careful. What if you had been in the carriage and were out of the city where the horses could go faster? I hate to think what may have happened."

Darcy placed his fingers over hers. "I will be. Of course, I will not leave the house until I am presentable, but even then, I will proceed with more caution."

Bingley looked at his friend. "You need to figure out who is doing these things. You cannot live like this, wondering from one day to the next what is going to drop out of the sky and land upon you."

"I agree with Mr. Bingley." Annabelle looked at Darcy. "These cannot be random events. Elizabeth has been blessed to so far avoid such attacks, but I fear for you both. Whoever this is, he must be stopped before one of you is seriously hurt, or killed."

Darcy hesitated, taking a deep breath before responding. "I know you are correct. I will try to figure out who could be behind the events."

The butler knocked on the door and, when Darcy bid him enter, slipped into the room with a silver salver in his hand.

"These letters just arrived, sir. The messenger did not wait. He has left the house."

Darcy could see in Mr. Baxter's features that something was odd about the notes. He thanked the man, took the missives off the salver, and dismissed him. As he looked at the directions, his brow creased.

"What is it, Darcy?" Colonel Fitzwilliam, his keen gaze trained upon his cousin, glanced between the envelopes and the other man's face.

Darcy licked his lips before he looked up. "There are no addresses on these, only names." He looked between the letters. "And … one is for Elizabeth."

Elizabeth startled, her eyes going wide. "What in the world? Who would send a letter to me here?" She accepted her note, looking at it as though it might bite her. She lifted her gaze to her betrothed's and chewed her lip.

Darcy took a deep breath. "I do not know, but I suppose we should find out. I do not recognize the handwriting, do you?"

She shook her head. "No."

"Well, then. Let us get it over with." Darcy broke the paste seal on his letter and slowly unfolded it while Elizabeth did the same with hers. He immediately looked at the bottom of the page to see it was unsigned. He moved back to the top to read the message when his betrothed gasped and dropped her missive.

"Lizzy!" Jane, who sat on her sister's other side, took hold of her hand. "Are you well?"

Darcy turned to see Elizabeth staring at the paper in her lap with one hand over her mouth and tears welling in her eyes. He snatched the sheet off her lap and began to read aloud.

Miss Elizabeth Bennet,

> *You were warned. And yet, you are even now in Mr. Darcy's house. You will pay for this and so will he. You should have heeded my words.*

Annabelle gasped as the gentlemen shouted. Darcy held up a hand.

"It is quite similar to mine. I will read it to you." He cleared his throat.

Mr. Darcy,

> *I see that nothing, not a beating or anything else, will keep you from ending*

> *your engagement to that trollop Elizabeth Bennet. You thought some bruised ribs and swollen eyes were bad. Wait until you experience what happens next. It will make you wish you had been killed in the attack.*

"Oh my word!" Elizabeth's horrified voice was the first to pierce the silence that descended upon the room. "What are we to do?" She shot to her feet. Her chin rose and she clenched her fists. "I will not allow this ... this ... *person* to intimidate me. He or she may do whatever they wish but I will not be cowed and I will *not* break my engagement!"

Darcy had jumped up when she did. He put his arm around her. No one seemed to notice the liberty he had taken. "I will not break it, either, I promise you." He squeezed her shoulder and tried to smile when she looked up at him. "We must take more precautions, I think. Clearly, for you to receive a note at my home, especially a threatening one, tells me that someone is watching one of us."

Fitzwilliam stood. "Hand those over here, Cousin." He accepted the letters and stepped away from the seating area, Bingley, Bennet, and Blackwell following.

"Perhaps some wine would be helpful right about now." Annabelle looked at Darcy, who nodded.

Just then, the butler announced dinner.

"Hang on a moment, Mr. Baxter." The colonel turned to Darcy and the rest of the guests. "I have a couple questions for your butler. The rest of you should go on ahead in to the dining room. I will not be long. Save me a glass of that port, Darcy. There's a good man." He winked at his cousin, who only shook his head.

"Very well. Do not be long. We will want to hear what you spoke about." Darcy removed his hand from Elizabeth's shoulder to hold his elbow out to her. When she had taken it, he led her out of the drawing room and down the hall, the rest of the group, save the colonel, behind them.

Darcy and his guests seated themselves in silence. They remained so while the first course was served. The tension could be felt, and the servants seemed to perform their duties as swiftly and silently as possible before disappearing. The atmosphere was relieved only when Fitzwilliam entered and took his seat.

"I am sorry for my unconventional behavior." The colonel picked up his glass and took a sip. "I asked Baxter if he had watched the direction in which the messenger walked when he left."

Darcy's brows rose. "And?"

Fitzwilliam took a spoonful of soup and swallowed before replying. "He thought the young man walked toward Bond Street."

Bennet had been listening closely. "That does not tell us much."

"It does not." The colonel shrugged. "It could have been anyone. Baxter says he was not dressed in livery, so I doubt he was a servant in one of the wealthier homes, though I suppose he could work in a house in Cheapside. Some tradesmen do very well and are able to hire footmen and maids."

"Yes." Jane agreed. "My aunt and uncle Gardiner have several servants. They do wear livery, though." She turned to Elizabeth. "Have we met any of their friends whose servants did not?"

Elizabeth shook her head. "Not that I can recall, but there may be others who do not do quite as well as our uncle." She shrugged. "However, I do concede that you and I have never witnessed such a thing."

"Well," Darcy said, his brow creased, "either way, I doubt he was a servant. It is common enough to hire boys along Bond Street to do odd jobs. He could have come all the way up from Cheapside, I would imagine. That is a long trip, though."

Bennet nodded. "For enough blunt, if he were like so many others, he would have willingly taken the trip." He picked up his glass and took a sip, looking over the rim with his brows raised.

"Very true." Blackwell leaned back. "I wish your butler had detained him. We may never discover the source of the letters without speaking to him."

"I agree, but unfortunately, what is done is done." Darcy fell silent as he noticed the footmen entering the room to remove the first course and serve the second. His guests followed suit and once the room had cleared again, the conversation turned to other things, though the letters and their threats were not far from anyone's mind.

Chapter 15

For the next several days, Darcy and Elizabeth, as well as her family, waited on tenterhooks to see what might happen. They were extremely cautious, never leaving the house alone and arming their footmen. They stayed in as much as possible, venturing out only as needed, or for a daily visit to Darcy House.

Darcy's bruised body healed quickly, for which both he and Elizabeth were thankful. Though he had searched his memory for anyone he may have offended enough to wish him harm, he could not identify anyone. The only person he had recently had words with was Sir Augustus Perry, and Darcy dismissed out of hand the idea that the baron could be behind the threatening letters and other events. He shook his head when his cousin questioned him about the man.

"He is a bully, I grant you, but as long as I have known him, he has been all talk. I have never heard of him doing anything in an underhanded manner."

Fitzwilliam seemed skeptical, lifting one brow while simultaneously frowning. "If you say so," he replied. "In my experience, anyone is capable of anything."

"Your experience has been in battle." Darcy waved a hand toward the window. "This is

London, not the continent."

The colonel pressed his lips together but did not push. "I hate to do this, but I must leave town. Father has called me to Rosings. I am uncertain why, but he wishes me to attend him as soon as possible. I have already requested a leave and my superiors have granted it. I will depart at dawn tomorrow." He paused. "I urge you not to discount the last letter you received. I know it has been over a week since it arrived, and a little longer than that since you were attacked, but it is entirely possible the miscreant responsible is simply biding his time."

"I will not ignore it. However, both Elizabeth and I are eager to get out of the house and reluctant to allow someone so wholly unconnected to us determine how we live our lives." He stood and walked to the window, looking out into the back garden. "I invited her to walk with me in Hyde Park on the morrow." He turned and took in his cousin's expression. "We will have an armed footman with us, I promise you. We will go early, before most of London is even out of bed, or at least, most of Mayfair. We will not traverse the entire park and will return before an hour is completed. We will be perfectly safe."

Fitzwilliam shook his head, then stood and approached Darcy as he spoke. "I wish you would not, but I know better than to insist otherwise." When he arrived at his cousin's side, he placed his hand on the man's shoulder. "Be careful. Remain aware of your surroundings. Do not become so lost in Miss Elizabeth's presence that you forget to keep watch."

"I will. I promise." The cousins shook hands, hugging briefly before the colonel said his farewells and left the house.

~~~***~~~

The next morning, Darcy, in his spare carriage, arrived at the Blackwell home just as the sun was beginning to rise. He waited for the groom to open the door, then stepped out, looking to his right and left to see if anyone was near. He looked at the servant and whispered a question.

"You have the pistol?"

The groom nodded, patting his waist, and Darcy knew the weapon was tucked inside the servant's waistband.

"I will return shortly. Keep your eyes open."

With a second nod, the other man shut the carriage door and stood alert, watching his employer being granted entrance to the house in between glances up and down the street.

A few minutes later, Darcy exited the home, this time with Elizabeth on his arm and a maid following. The three entered the equipage and within seconds, he had knocked on the ceiling to tell the coachman to move. The carriage lurched into motion.

Bruton Street, like Brooke Street, was only a short drive from Hyde Park. At an early hour such as this, the traffic was light and the trip was brief. When they reached the entrance, and the equipage came once more to a stop, Darcy exited, handing his betrothed down. The footman was to follow the couple, and so the maid elected to remain with the carriage and climbed up to chat with Mr. Drover. Darcy tucked Elizabeth's hand under his elbow and they set off, strolling down the footpath.

"Thank you for this invitation." Elizabeth looked around the beautifully laid out park. "It is so peaceful here at this time of day." She lifted her face to take in the rays of the barely-risen sun.

"I remembered you telling me how much you enjoyed early-morning walks at your home. Now that I am healed enough to leave my house, I thought it was the perfect way to spend time with you. I confess I was eager to bring you here." He brought his free hand up to rest over hers where it was curled around his arm.

The cry of a flock of geese rising from the Serpentine drew their attention and they paused for a couple minutes to watch. Then, they continued on their way. They chatted now and again about things they had seen, but much of their walk was passed in a comfortable silence. Finally, as they entered a thick copse of trees, Darcy pulled out his watch and noted the time.

"We have been walking close to a half-hour." He stopped, and Elizabeth let go of his arm. "We should head back." He turned and paused, his brow creasing as he looked down the path. "Where did Jeremiah go? He was told to remain in sight of us." Offering his arm to his betrothed, he added, "Let us find him. I cannot think what might have caused him to abandon his post."

Before Darcy and Elizabeth could take a step, a figure leaped out of the woods, brandishing a pistol at them.

"Stay where you are."

The couple froze, Elizabeth gasping as Darcy stiffened. It took no more than a heartbeat to identify the man before them.

"What do you think you are doing, sir?" Darcy used his most commanding voice, not believing that the gentleman before him was actually capable of shooting someone.

Sir Augustus Perry sneered at his rival. "What does it look like I am doing? I am separating you from Miss Elizabeth Bennet. You have been warned multiple times and yet, you persist in refusing to break your betrothal." He waved the pistol. "Remove yourself from her."

Darcy felt Elizabeth clutch his arm tighter and rested his free hand over hers. "What do you mean when you say I have been warned? You have not approached me for weeks. I told you then that I was firm in my decision to marry her. Though she does not lay the blame for her compromise at my feet, I was the gentleman whose name was negatively linked with hers. I will not leave her to suffer the whims of society alone." He squeezed her hand. "Besides, I have come to find her to be everything delightful. I believe we shall do very well together. I will not give her up." He felt his betrothed hug his arm in response, though he ignored it to focus on the man in front of them.

Perry laughed. "Have you not connected recent events together yet? Letters, a beating, your carriage? A shame you were not involved in that last." He shook his head. "One cannot rely on employees to take the same care to do things that one themselves would. I should have dealt with matters myself instead of hiring others to do them for me."

Darcy felt his heart pounding. He strove to display a calm demeanor and not let his feelings show. To hear Sir Augustus admit to being behind the intimidation he and Elizabeth had been subjected to was chilling. He thought quickly, not wishing the baron to see the alarm he felt at the thought of Elizabeth being hurt or, possibly worse, under the man's control. He needed to get the pistol away from the man, and soon. He wondered again where Jeremiah had gotten to.

"A gentleman does not behave as you have." Darcy sniffed, attempting to appear nonchalant. "When word of this gets around, you will lose what standing you do have, which is not much." He looked the other man up and down. "And trust me, word *will* get around. I will see to it myself."

Sir Augustus turned red, his smug smile turning instantly into a glower. "No," he growled in reply, "you will not." He cocked the hammer on the gun. "Since you still refuse to let go of my betrothed, I will separate you. Permanently."

Elizabeth had watched the confrontation unfold with growing horror and not a little anger. Now, seeing the man she had rejected point his weapon at Darcy's heart and pull the hammer back, she knew only one thing: that she must save the gentleman she had grown to love. She pulled away from Darcy and threw herself in front of him. "No!" she shouted. "Do not shoot him." She held her hands up, ignoring his exclamations behind her. "I will go with you if you promise me you will not shoot him."

The baron sneered. "Well, is that not sweet? What have you done, fall in love with him?" He shook his head. "That is terrible for you, but I intend to make sure you forget him. At least, until I send you to join him in the dark silence of death." He stepped forward and grabbed her arm, attempting to yank her forward.

Elizabeth resisted, digging her heels in. "I will not go with you unless you promise not to kill him." She felt Darcy wrap his arms around her waist and leaned into his strength, preventing Sir Augustus from pulling her away.

Suddenly, it seemed the struggle was over. The baron let go and released the hammer of his pistol without firing. "Very well, then." He turned the weapon over in his hand, holding it by the barrel and showing her the stock. "I can no longer fire. I will leave him alive. However, you *will* come with me. Immediately."

Elizabeth stilled, as did her betrothed behind her. She swallowed, knowing she must now keep her word but dreading letting Darcy go. She turned to search his gaze with her own, trying to convey to him the depth of her feelings. "All will be well," she whispered to him. "I will return to you as soon as I can. I promise."

"What are you saying?" Perry grabbed her arm and yanked her back. Then, he stepped toward Darcy while the other man's focus was still on Elizabeth, drew back the hand that held the barrel of the pistol, and smashed the stock against his head. Darcy dropped like a stone, making the baron grin. Next, he turned back toward his soon-to-be-wife, who had cried out and now sobbed, trying to reach Darcy, and struck her with the back of his hand. "Shut up. You are mine and I forbid you from crying over another man." Without another word, he shoved her into the trees. Roughly, he pushed and pulled her to the other side of the copse and into the carriage that was waiting on another path.

Elizabeth sobbed as she struggled to remain on her feet. Seeing her betrothed struck down like that had been terrifying. She silently prayed that he would be well. When she and her captor arrived at his equipage, she closed her eyes, swallowed, and entered as Sir Augustus directed. Her reticule thumped against her leg and she remembered the small, single shot pistol her uncle had taught her and Jane to use just a week ago. The reminder that she was not completely unprotected soothed her heart. She vowed to herself that she would get out of this situation one way or another. Her uncle's words rang in her mind.

> *"You have only one opportunity to use this weapon. Choose your moment carefully, and aim for the place on your assailant's body where the most damage will be done. Remember, you will not likely kill him; your goal is to injure him enough that you can escape."*

Her tears began to dry as she tried to pay more attention to the man who had taken her. The windows of the carriage were covered, so not only was she unable to see where they were going, she could not see Sir Augustus clearly, either. Still, she could listen, and as they travelled, she noticed the level and types of sounds changing. She could tell they were no longer in Mayfair, though she was uncertain in which part of London they now were.

Eventually, the coach stopped and Sir Augustus exited, pulling her out behind him and hustling her inside a building without giving her time to look around or get her bearings. He dragged her up a set of stairs and into a sparsely-furnished room with boarded-up windows. He threw her toward the bed in the corner.

"I have some things to take care of, but I will be back. Escape is impossible."

Elizabeth stood, her spine stiff and her chin raised. "I will not marry you willingly."

Perry laughed. "Oh, yes, you will." He took a step toward her. "You see, I intend to keep you here for a day or two and tell every gossip I know that you are with me. Your reputation will be so ruined by the time I let you go that you will have to either marry me or be considered a light-skirt, a wanton Cyprian, fit for nothing but a brothel." He came another step closer, reaching his finger out to run down her cheek, a strange look coming into his eye. "Of course, I will have had you by then, and you will no doubt desire more of me." He scowled when she flinched away from him. Shoving her backwards and causing her to fall, he towered over her and shouted. "Perhaps Darcy has been before me and ruined my enjoyment, eh? Maybe I will take what I want and kill you instead of marrying you." He paused, chest heaving.

Elizabeth remained silent, alert and wary. When he finally moved away, she breathed a quiet sigh of relief. *Not while I have breath in my body,* she thought as she watched him walk out of the room. She closed her eyes and held back tears as the door shut and she heard the lock click.

Chapter 16

Darcy groaned as awareness seeped into his consciousness. He opened his eyes, blinking as the light hit them. He wondered where he was for just a second, before the memory struck him. "Elizabeth!"

He stumbled to his feet, looking around with one hand pressed to his head where the butt of the gun had struck him. Seeing that his betrothed was gone, as was Sir Augustus, he began to stagger down the path in the direction he had come earlier. Just around a bend several feet away, he found the body of his footman. He could see that the man was dead; his eyes stared sightlessly and a thin cord was still wrapped around his neck. Darcy opened the servant's coat and removed the gun from his waistband. He paused a moment to pray for the man's family but staggered to his feet once more and made his way to the park entrance as swiftly as his aching and bleeding head would allow him to.

He was within sight of his destination when he heard John Drover call out to him. A few seconds later, the coachman was at his side.

"Sir! What happened? Are you well? Where is Miss Elizabeth?" Drover glanced behind his employer. "Where is Jeremiah?"

"Miss Elizabeth has been kidnapped and

Jeremiah is dead. Come, we must go to Blackwell's house and inform him and call the magistrate." Darcy leaned heavily against his driver. The man took his weight without complaint and guided him to the carriage door. Within moments, the horses were whipped up and they were moving around the park, headed back to Bruton Street.

Traffic had increased while Darcy and Elizabeth had been in the park, so the trip back to her uncle's home took much longer than the earlier one had. Darcy fought nausea and pain as he clung to the strap and tried to remain on the seat. His only thought was his betrothed and how to find her. He closed his eyes and let out a huge breath when the carriage stopped. He pulled himself together and, when the door opened, stumbled down to the pavement. His coachman grabbed his arm, holding him up, and together with the maid, who had taken his other arm, they got him up the shallow steps. Drover knocked on the door.

The heavy wood panel opened. Somerset's jaw went slack as he took in Darcy's condition. "Come in, sir." He stood back to allow the other man to enter, snapping his fingers at Mrs. West, who was hovering nearby, and gesturing toward the back of the house. Instantly, the housekeeper turned and scurried away.

Darcy stood as straight as he could and began issuing commands. "I need to speak to Blackwell at once, and the magistrate and runners must be summoned."

"I will send someone right away." Somerset bowed. "Let me see you to the drawing room. The master will be here momentarily."

Darcy nodded but said nothing. He followed the butler to the drawing room door and was about to enter when he heard Blackwell's voice hailing him.

"Darcy! What has happened?" He looked around. "Where is my niece?"

Darcy gestured inside the room. "Some privacy would be best." He entered and made his way to the nearest seat, a wingback chair in the middle of the room, and collapsed into it.

Blackwell stopped in front of his butler. "Somerset, have someone bring in warm water and some towels. Be prepared to call the physician. Oh, and when Mr. Bennet returns, send him to me."

Somerset bowed again. "Mr. Darcy has requested the magistrate and runners be called, as well."

Blackwell nodded. "Very good. See to it at once."

With another bow, the butler silently shut the door behind his employer and hastened to do as he had been ordered.

Inside the drawing room, Blackwell approached the younger man. His brow was creased. "Tell me what has happened." He perched on the edge of a chair next to Darcy's.

"Sir Augustus Perry accosted us as we were heading back to the carriage. He was armed." Darcy shook his head. "He must have knocked me out; Elizabeth had spoken to me and I was about to reply when everything went black." He paused when the door opened and a pair of maids brought in the water and towels.

Blackwell ordered a tea tray and waited for the girls to leave. He then looked at Darcy. "Continue, please."

"When I came to, Elizabeth and Perry were gone. I started back toward my carriage and found my groom lying off the side of the path. He had been strangled." Darcy closed his eyes. "Elizabeth threw herself between me and the baron. She sacrificed herself to save me." Tears welled up and he swallowed, trying to control them.

Blackwell was speechless. His mouth opened and closed several times. Finally, he found words. "I am shocked. You are certain, absolutely certain, it was Sir Augustus who did this?"

Darcy swallowed and opened his eyes. "I am. He did not bother to conceal his features. In fact, he gloated about having us at his mercy." He went on to give the details of the encounter.

Blackwell stood and paced to the window as he struggled to control his anger. The maids entered again with tea things and the gentlemen remained silent. When they had gone, he spoke.

"Somerset has called for the magistrate and runners, as you requested." He walked over to Darcy and looked at his head, which had mostly stopped bleeding. "Come over here and wash up so I can see if we need the physician." When the younger man pushed up to his feet, he caught his gaze. "I do not blame you for this event. You took precautions and did exactly as you promised you would. I cannot say how Bennet will react, though, so be prepared."

Darcy nodded and made his way to the ewer. He was washing his face when the butler knocked on the drawing room door again.

"Sir, Mr. Bingley and Miss Bingley are here to speak to Mr. Darcy."

Blackwell glanced at his guest, who had straightened and was wiping his cheek with the towel. "Bring them in."

Somerset nodded, bowed, and retreated. Blackwell approached Darcy to examine his head. "You need to sit for this. You are far too tall for me to see your head well."

Darcy approached his seat again but before he reached it, Somerset appeared once more, with Bingley and Caroline in tow.

"Darcy! What happened to you?" Bingley's usual cheerful tone was replaced with one of concern.

"Please be seated." Blackwell gestured to

the sofa nearby. "Our friend here needs to sit before he falls over."

The guests seated themselves and Darcy explained to his friend the events of the morning. He paid no mind to Caroline when she gasped and her hand rose to cover her mouth.

Bingley's eyes widened as he listened. When Darcy was done, he explained the reason he had brought Miss Bingley along. "Caroline came to me this morning with quite a tale. I hesitated to believe her, but clearly, she must have been correct." He turned to his sister. "Tell them what you told me."

Caroline nodded, sitting straighter in her seat. "I attended Lady Jemima's card party last night. There was a gentleman there speaking to someone else. I overheard their conversation. I do not think they realized how loud their voices were." She paused, looking down, and took a deep breath. "The first gentleman was saying he was going to separate the woman he wished to marry from someone who refused to give her up. He said he planned to take her from her family and keep her at a house he owns in Coleman Street in Cheapside for a few days so her family would be forced to allow her to marry him. The second gentleman seemed to be trying to discourage him, but the first said he would not be thwarted by anyone, even if that person was a Darcy and of the highest circles."

Darcy's mien was dark. He did not trust

Caroline Bingley and remained angry with her for treating Elizabeth so poorly. "Why should I believe you?" He turned to his friend. "I am sorry. I mean no offense to you."

Bingley rushed to reassure his friend. "No, no, I am not offended. I reacted the same way."

Darcy nodded and then his implacable gaze returned to Caroline. "I ask again: why should I believe you?"

Caroline shifted in her seat but then her chin lifted and she looked him in the eyes. "I wish to keep my reputation intact, and to maintain my connection to you and your family. I realize that my cold behavior toward Miss Bennet and Miss Elizabeth did me no favors." She sniffed and glanced away, her chin lifting even higher. "You clearly have no desire to marry a woman like me and I cannot change that." She looked back at Darcy. "But a connection to you would allow me to meet more gentlemen of your ilk who might be willing to. By informing you of what I heard last night, I am hoping to make up for last week's mistakes and get back into your good graces."

Darcy had observed carefully while she spoke and believed she was sincere. He leaned back. "I am shocked at your brutal honesty, but I can see that you are not dissembling. Your information is invaluable to us. Thank you."

Caroline pressed her lips together and nodded her acknowledgement of his words but said nothing else.

At that point, the runners and magistrate arrived, both at the same time. Bingley sent his sister home in their carriage and re-entered the drawing room as the investigators, Blackwell, and Darcy shared information and came up with a plan.

Blackwell finally found the opportunity to look at Darcy's wound. "It is not gaping, thankfully. I do not believe it will need stitches, but we should perhaps pour some brandy over it to help it heal. I have a bottle stashed in the wine cellar. It will have to last until the war on the continent is over, so we will need to be sparing with it, but my grandfather swore by it."

Darcy grimaced. "Very well. I will allow it, as long as you give me a drink of it first. My father believed the same. I well remember what alcohol in an open wound feels like."

The men all laughed, but soon, were wincing in sympathy with Darcy. Once his head was cleaned up, all but Blackwell piled into his carriage and headed out to look for the house Caroline had spoken of.

~~~***~~~

Elizabeth paced back and forth in the small room, as she had done the majority of the time since she had been locked in it. She paused when she reached the bed, lifting the pillow to check the pistol she had hidden there. Reassured that the hammer was cocked and that it was ready to fire at a moment's notice, she resumed her pacing.

Only a few minutes later, she heard footsteps on the stairs. She rushed to sit on the bed next to her hidden weapon, sliding her hand under the pillow to grasp the stock. Glancing down, she made sure her skirts covered her wrist. She held herself rigid with chin lifted as Sir Augustus entered the room, closing the door behind him.

"What? You will not stand when I enter?" His voice mocked her. "I bet if I were Darcy you would have been on your feet." He sneered as he stepped toward her, stopping only inches away. "I went back to finish him off, you know." He laughed when she gasped. "Did you seriously believe I would allow him to live after he refused to let you go?" He shrugged. "He was not there, but it is of small importance at the moment. I will kill him later. I have much more pressing business on my mind."

Elizabeth forced herself not to cringe when the baron leaned toward her. She looked in the direction of the boarded up window, biding her time and looking for her moment. Her uncle's voice floated through her mind, telling her that she must be close to her attacker for the pistol to be effective.

Sir Augustus kissed her ear, and Elizabeth shuddered involuntarily. She was unable to prevent a grimace from passing across her

179

features. She hoped he did not see it, but he must have, because he suddenly cursed and shoved her back on the bed, crawling on top of her. It was now or never, she knew.

Elizabeth pulled her hand, holding the pistol, out from under the pillow and slipped it between them, pressing it against his chest as he came closer. She closed her eyes and pulled the trigger.

Sir Augustus jerked backwards, a look of surprise on his face. He looked down at himself and then lifted his head toward her before slumping forward.

Elizabeth screamed as his heavy weight landed on her. She shoved at him and wiggled, trying to get out from under him. She sobbed, tears streaming from her eyes, down the sides of her face and into her hair. Forcing herself to calm, she realized that the baron was lying half on the bed and that one more good push should do. She took a deep breath and shoved with all her might and was suddenly free. She jumped up and ran for the door.

Within a few minutes, she was on the street. She stopped and looked both ways. She did not recognize anything and had no idea where to go. However, she was not going to stay where she was. She chose a direction and began to run, ignoring the gasps, pointed fingers, and screams that her bloodied and disheveled appearance elicited.

All at once, someone was before her calling

her name. He stopped her headlong flight, taking hold of her upper arms.

"Elizabeth!"

She screamed and struck out, blinded by her shock and fear and not recognizing him.

"Elizabeth, it is me, Darcy. It is over."

She felt herself pulled into his arms. She whimpered. "Mr. Darcy?"

"Yes, my love. Look at me."

A finger lifted her chin and she looked up into his concerned gaze. "I-, he-" She stuttered, trying to tell him what had happened, but was unable to form the words.

"Shh. All is well. Tell me later."

Elizabeth nodded and melted into Darcy's embrace. She heard him order someone to bring the carriage and heard another voice ask if anyone had seen which house she had exited. She heard the clop of horses' hooves on the cobblestones and then the sound of someone opening a door.

Darcy looked down at the woman covered in blood in his arms and knew she was in shock. When the coachman opened the door, he bent to place an arm behind her knees and lift her into the carriage. He placed her on a seat and lifted the one opposite, pulling out two thick rugs kept there for travel in colder weather. He wrapped her in one, picked her up and placed her on his lap, and covered them both with the other. By the time he was

181

thus settled, Bingley had returned and was ascending into the equipage.

"They found him." The man tipped his head toward Elizabeth. "She shot him in the heart." He pulled a small pistol out of his pocket. "This is the weapon. I do not know if it was a lucky shot or if she is that good, but he had to have been dead within seconds."

Darcy squeezed Elizabeth tightly. "Thank heavens for that. Was he clothed?"

"He was. He was on a bed, though. There is not a doubt in my mind what he planned, given his position and the location of the wound."

With a nod, Darcy kissed his betrothed's hair. "I need to get her home. She needs to see a physician."

"The runners are conducting their investigation and calling the undertaker; they have given us leave to go whenever you are ready to." Bingley nodded toward Elizabeth once more. "A shot of something strong will go a long way toward making her right again."

Darcy moved a hand away from his betrothed to reach into his inner coat pocket. "I have brandy. It will do." He pulled a flask out and used the fingers of the hand still holding Elizabeth to twist the top open. Then, he held the bottle to her lips.

"Here, darling. Take a sip." He urged her to drink, sighing in relief when she did, then making her take a second sip after she coughed. "It will warm you. Come, now." He forced a third sip into her and then stoppered the bottle and replaced it. Telling Bingley to have the coachman take them to Bruton Street, he settled in for the ride, speaking softly to Elizabeth and running his hand up and down her arm.

Chapter 17

Darcy descended from the carriage in front of the Blackwell home with Elizabeth in his arms. He did not feel the least bit guilty for holding her in his lap the entire trip. She was going to be his wife as soon as it could be arranged and if anyone thought less of either of them, that person would not be welcomed in their lives any longer. He carried her, still wrapped in one of the blankets, into her uncle's house.

Blackwell met him in the foyer, Bennet on his heels. "Is she well?"

"She is unhurt, but she has suffered a shock." Darcy did not wait to allow the gentlemen to look at her. Instead, he turned toward the drawing room, walking past them and into the short hallway and leaving Bingley to explain what had happened.

The butler sped past and opened the door, standing aside as Darcy carried his burden into the room and settled her on the sofa.

Blackwell stepped out of the way of his brother-in-law to give his senior servant some instructions. "Inform my niece's maid that she will need bathwater and clean clothing. Ask Mrs. West to bring a tray with tea and chocolate and some of those raspberry scones that Elizabeth liked so much this morning. I will ring you if we need anything else."

"Very good, sir." The butler bowed, leaving with haste to do as instructed.

On the other side of the drawing room, Darcy had moved out of the way so Bennet could speak to his daughter.

"Lizzy, I am here." Bennet ran his hand over her hair, brushing it off her forehead and smoothing it back.

"Papa?" Elizabeth blinked opened her eyes. "Where is Mr. Darcy? What have you done with him?"

Bennet chuckled through his tears. "I have done nothing with him. He is here, as well." He turned around to locate the young man and then looked back at his favorite child. "He is watching over my shoulder. If you keep your eyes open long enough, you will see him."

Darcy cleared his throat. "I gave her some brandy in the carriage. She might be sleepy."

Bennet shook his head. "Are you drunk, my dear?"

Elizabeth forced her eyes open. "I do not know. Perhaps?" She closed her eyes and began to whisper to her father. "I killed him, Papa." She started to cry.

Bennet swallowed. "I know. I am sorry you had to do that."

She sniffed. "I am not. He was going to kill the man I love, and me, too. I could not allow that to happen." She cried harder.

Bennet chafed her hand. "You are a brave

young lady and I love you all the more for it."

Darcy cleared his throat. "The tray has been brought in. Miss Elizabeth, a bit of tea or chocolate might make you feel better. Having something in my stomach always makes my mind feel clearer, I find."

"Do you want some chocolate, my child? I believe I see some scones on the tray, as well." Bennet caressed her hand some more.

Elizabeth's eyes opened. "Chocolate would be nice." She wiped her eyes on her sleeve as her father helped her sit up. "Oh." She looked down at herself, seeing her bloody gown and gasping.

Darcy took charge when Blackwell and Bennet both began staring at the red stain on her chest. "If you would rather, we can have the tray taken to your chambers and you can bathe and change your gown while you drink it."

With shaking hands, Elizabeth gathered the blanket up around her and sniffed, her chin quivering. "I will drink a cup now. I do not feel up to standing. I will take the rest with me, though."

Darcy nodded and served her the thick dark liquid, stirring in sugar and cream as she requested. By then, the other gentlemen had shaken themselves out of their stupor and were pouring themselves glasses of port.

Elizabeth drank half her cup of chocolate, then set it down and asked to be escorted to her rooms. Her father quickly agreed and soon

187

she was in a steaming bath, doing her best to scrub herself clean.

~~~***~~~

Darcy and Bingley returned to Darcy House once his betrothed was taken upstairs. Blackwell had assured them before they left that they were welcome to come back later and dine with them, and that he was sure Elizabeth and Jane would want to see them.

"I will have to write to my cousin and tell him about this." Darcy collapsed into a chair in his study and waved his friend into another. "He will be furious. He warned me not to take her to the park and I assured him we would be perfectly safe with an armed guard." He shook his head. "Such hubris. Fitzwilliam will skewer me over it, though not as badly as I am berating myself."

"You could not know what he had planned, though. You did what you thought was best. How could you have predicted that the man would kill an innocent servant to get to you?"

Darcy held his glass to his forehead and rolled it across. "I could not. I should have, though. We both received letters threatening violence and I ignored them. Elizabeth could have been killed because of my negligence." He threw back the alcohol and slammed the glass on the table before shoving himself to his feet to march toward the fireplace. "I swore to protect her. I *promised* her I would. And instead, I led her right to the fiend who threatened her." He slammed his fist on the top of the mantel. "It is inexcusable."

"You are taking too much on yourself. I am certain Miss Elizabeth does not blame you. I certainly do not." Bingley paused. "Did you know Blackwell taught both Bennet girls to shoot the other day? He took them to a field outside of London, gave each of them one of those single-shot pistols, and gave them lessons on how to load, cock, and shoot them, as well as how to clean them. Jane told me she was frightened nearly to death to even hold one but her sister was fearless with it."

Darcy closed his eyes and sighed before turning to face his friend. "I was unaware of the details but I did know he had taught them the basics. I will be forever grateful he took that step. There is not a doubt in my mind that those lessons saved Elizabeth's life."

Bingley tilted his head and studied his friend. "Have you told her of your feelings? That you love her?"

Darcy did not immediately reply, instead walking back to his chair and slowly lowering himself into it. He leaned his head against the back and closed his eyes again. "Not yet," he whispered. "I wanted to wait until I was more certain of her feelings. Then this happened, and when I found her, my mind was too full of comforting her and making sure she was well to even think of it. Of course, once we arrived at her uncle's home, he and her father were there and I could not."

Bingley chuckled. "No, you could not, not in front of her father. You will soon, though."

"I will. Tonight, if I can get her alone for a few minutes." He rolled his head toward his friend. "That sounded very much like a command and not a suggestion, you know."

Bingley flushed but smirked. "Call it what you like as long as you follow it."

Darcy rolled his eyes with an answering grin, then closed them as he moved his face away once more. He sighed.

"You look terrible. Perhaps you should go up to your rooms and rest if you wish to see Miss Elizabeth again today." Bingley stood. "I need to go home, as well. Shall I pick you up or go directly to Blackwell's?"

Darcy dragged himself to his feet. "Come here. We can ride together." He led his friend into the hall and to the front door. "Thank you for everything you did today." He clapped Bingley on the shoulder. "I could not have survived the day without you."

"It was nothing. You would have done the same if our positions were reversed." Bingley stretched out his hand and shook Darcy's. "I will see you later."

When the door shut behind his friend, Darcy informed Mr. Baxter that he was not to be disturbed the remainder of the afternoon and trudged up the stairs, eager to bathe and rest his aching head. Smith had steaming water already filling the tub when he arrived in his rooms and soon, Darcy was clean and dressed in fresh clothing. He stretched out on the bed, falling instantly into sleep.

~~~***~~~

That evening, Darcy and Bingley entered the Blackwells' house rested and refreshed. Darcy's head still ached a bit and, when touched, caused him a deal of pain. However, he was determined to see Elizabeth and assure himself that she was well. When they were announced, he entered on Somerset's heels, eagerly looking for her. His steps faltered when he realized she was not present.

"Welcome, gentlemen." Blackwell bowed. "Come in and sit."

Darcy did as he was invited to, but could not keep himself from asking about his betrothed. "Where is Elizabeth? Is she well?"

His host hesitated before replying. "She is as well as can be expected. She did not get much rest this afternoon. We called the physician to look at her. He prescribed laudanum, though she refused to take it." He shrugged. "She wanted to see you. She has promised to take some tonight to help her sleep. My wife and Jane are up with her, getting her ready to come down."

Darcy's brow creased. "Why did she not rest?"

Bennet replied before his brother could. "Every time she fell asleep, she had a nightmare. Jane and Annabelle have spent the entire afternoon with her, but even their presence could not keep the demons away."

"I see." Darcy looked at his feet as he thought. "The nightmares ... they were of the shooting?" He lifted his eyes again to search Bennet's face for clues.

"I believe so. The ladies were not specific and I have not spoken to them directly." Bennet paused. "She called out for you, as I understand it. She has developed a strong attachment to you."

Darcy's eyes widened. "I did not know that, but I am happy to hear it. I have done the same. It tears me up to know that she suffers."

Bennet nodded and was silent for another minute or two as he examined the younger man. Finally, he spoke again. "At first, I was angered that Elizabeth was put in danger when she was with you, who had promised us all that you would keep her safe, but the more I thought about it and the more my brother spoke of your agony when you arrived here without her, the more I realized that you did all you could to assure her safety. I want to be certain you understand that I do not hold this incident against you. Everything you have done since the day the two of you met has been completed with an eye to her care and well-being. You could not have foreseen the events of this morning. I do not believe I could give her to a better man." He stood and approached Darcy, who had also risen, and held out his hand. "Welcome to the family." The gentlemen shook hands.

"Thank you, sir. It is an honor." Anything else Darcy would have said was cut off, because at that moment, the door opened and the ladies entered.

"Good evening, gentlemen." Annabelle approached the seating area with Jane and Elizabeth behind her, their arms linked.

Darcy, along with Bingley, Blackwell, and Bennet, bowed. As soon as he straightened, Darcy stepped forward to reach for Elizabeth's hands.

"Are you well?" It was all he could do to keep from caressing her wan cheek.

Elizabeth squeezed his hands and gave him a wavery smile. "I had trouble sleeping, but I am better now."

Darcy smiled back as his gaze roamed her features. His thumbs caressed the backs of her hands. "Will you sit beside me and talk for a moment?" His head snapped up and he addressed her father. "Might Miss Elizabeth and I have a bit of private conversation?" He nodded toward the end of the room, where a chaise lounge was positioned in front of the window. "Over there?"

Bennet's smile was indulgent. "You may,

yes." He nodded to his blushing daughter and turned to retake his seat.

Darcy smiled shyly at his betrothed and tucked one of her hands under his elbow. He led her across the room and gently seated her on the chaise, taking up a spot beside her and turning so he faced her.

"Elizabeth, today ..." He trailed off as he fought back a sudden onslaught of emotion. "Over the course of the last weeks, I have come to understand the kind of female you are: honorable, kind, generous, and loving. I have witnessed your care for your family and friends, and ... me ... even to the point where you would sacrifice yourself, your future, and your happiness. When I saw the baron standing in front of us today, brandishing a weapon, I feared for us both. My entire focus was on keeping you safe. Then, when you threw yourself between us and bartered for my life ..." He stopped again as tears once more threatened. He swallowed. "I was terrified," he finally whispered. "I rejoiced when I found you on that street and I vowed to myself to never be parted from you again." He paused. "Elizabeth, I have grown to love you in a way I never thought I would be capable of. Almost from the first time I saw you, you impressed me with the fullest belief of your innocence, your honesty, and your selfless trust in others. I have not known you a month complete, but in that time, you have become the only woman in the world I could ever be prevailed upon to marry.

Thank you for accepting me. I love you."

Elizabeth's feelings on hearing Darcy's words had swelled within her and overflowed into joyful tears that tracked down her cheeks. When he finally completed his declaration, there was nothing she could do except to retrieve one of her hands from his grasp and use it to cup his cheek. "My heart soars at your words, because I feel the same. I love you, so very much. Thank you for offering for me. You have turned a time of fear and distress into the most cherished moments of my life."

Darcy's hand had come up to cover hers and press it to his cheek. Now, he turned his face into it to bestow a kiss on the palm. "You have made me the happiest of men." He retained his grasp of her hands, twining his fingers with hers and resting them on his knees.

Chapter 18

A cough from across the room caught Darcy's attention, and he and Elizabeth both looked over to see her father and uncle watching them. He looked down to hide a smile and turned his attention back to his betrothed, who had done the same thing. "Come," he said as he stood, bringing her up with him. "We should join the others."

Darcy took a single step and then stopped, causing Elizabeth to do the same. "I meant it when I said I never wish to be parted from you again. I have the special license. We can marry at any time now. All that is needed is to choose a date and engage the clergyman." He searched her eyes. "What say you to Friday?"

"Four days from now?" Elizabeth's brow creased as she thought. Finally, her expression cleared. "I think that is an excellent idea. I do not need much to prepare. My trousseau has already been ordered and I have a gown you have not seen that can serve as my wedding dress." She glanced toward the other side of the room. "Shall we announce it?"

A relieved, happy smile spread across Darcy's face. He tucked her hand under his arm, again linking the fingers of his free hand with hers. "We shall."

As they approached, Annabelle noted their

happy countenances. She smiled at them. "I think your conversation must have been a productive one."

"It was." Elizabeth glanced at Darcy. "We have chosen a wedding date."

Bennet's brows rose. "Oh? And, what date did you choose?"

Darcy cleared his throat. "Friday of this week." He waited for the gasps and expressions of surprise to pass. "We do not wish to be apart any longer than we have to be, not after the events of this morning. Elizabeth assures me everything is in readiness and shares my feelings about waiting."

"Well, then, congratulations to you both." Bennet stepped closer to his daughter and kissed her cheek. "What of your mother and sisters? Do you wish for them to attend?"

Elizabeth hesitated, biting her lip and looking up at Darcy.

"I know what you and all your family have expressed to me about your mother, but truly, my love, it is you I am marrying and – forgive me, Mr. Bennet – Derbyshire is far from Hertfordshire; if she really is so difficult to bear, we need not do it often. If you wish for her to come, I will send my coach to pick her up. Your sisters, as well, of course."

"I have always imagined my entire family being with me when I went through such a momentous event."

"Then it is settled." Darcy turned to Bennet. "My traveling coach is at your disposal, sir."

"I thank you." Bennet bowed. "And you, as well, Lizzy. Your mother would be very disappointed to miss your wedding. I am happy that I do not have to listen to her complaints." He winked at his daughter. "I appreciate the offer of your coach, Mr. Darcy, but my brother has one and I had already requested it for just such an instance."

At that moment, Somerset interrupted to announce the meal, and the group strolled in pairs down to the dining room. They seated themselves informally, as Annabelle had instructed them to do, and soon were spooning up a rich broth with vegetables. Once the edge had been taken off their hunger, conversation began to arise.

Jane looked between her father, her uncle, and Darcy. "What will happen about Sir Augustus as far as Lizzy goes? Will there be legal repercussions for her?"

Elizabeth stiffened, and Darcy reached for her hand under the table, squeezing it and then retaining a tight grip on it to assure her she was not alone.

Blackwell leaned forward, clasping his hands and resting his wrists on the edge of the table. "The magistrate visited the house this afternoon. We ..." He gestured toward Bennet with a glance in the other man's direction. "... pressed upon him the importance of keeping Lizzy's name out of it. It has been de-cided that the investigation will simply declare that an unknown assailant killed him. It is doubtful that anyone will look into the issue too closely. Perry had few friends and no fami-ly that anyone knows of."

"What of the people on the street who saw Miss Elizabeth running away?"

Bennet leaned back in his seat as he an-swered. "Elizabeth is unknown in that area, Mr. Bingley. It is doubtful she ever sees any of them again, or them her. The risk of her iden-tity becoming known is small."

Bingley nodded. "Ture," he murmured. He looked down to where he was tracing the bottom of his glass with his finger. "That is a relief."

Jane looked from Bingley to her father. "I am happy it can be so arranged. I have been terrified at the thought of my dearest sister going to prison, or worse."

Elizabeth shuddered then, an action that she could not control but that everyone at the table witnessed.

"I think we all are, Miss Bennet," Darcy said as he fought the almost overwhelming urge to pull his betrothed closer and hold her. She clearly needed him to, but this was not the time or the place for that. Instead, he tightened his grasp on her hand and, when she lifted her face to his, put all the assurance he could into his smile. He was relieved when she smiled back and seemed to relax.

The rest of the evening passed in a pleasant manner, with no more discussion of Sir Augustus Perry or the horrors Darcy and Elizabeth had suffered that day.

~~~***~~~

The following morning, as Darcy was dealing with his post, Mr. Baxter knocked on his door.

"This letter just arrived, sir. Lord Matlock's personal messenger brought it." The butler extended the salver to his master.

Darcy picked the note up off the tray and dismissed the servant. He immediately broke the seal and began to read.

Darcy,

We have received your invitation for the wedding on Friday. I was horrified by the tale you told, but I will not say "I told you so." Though, I did. Tell you so. Anyway, I have informed my parents, and they are just as distressed as I have been. They told me to extend to you their gratitude for your good health, as well as that of your betrothed.

Father assures me that he will keep an ear out for any gossip regarding Sir Augustus Perry's demise and the person responsible. He and Mother will do eve-

rything they can to make sure Elizabeth's name is not connected to it in any manner.

We did not inform Anne of the events you related to us. We only told her of the date of your wedding. She asked me to extend her congratulations to you both.

I might as well tell you now as to wait. You will discover it before the week is out, anyway. I have proposed to Anne and she has accepted me. My parents pushed for me to do it, but it was Anne who finally decided me. She confessed to me that you had been correct when you said she likes me better than you. She has harbored a secret tendre for me for years, it seems, but her mother was so set on her marrying you that she feared we could never be together. So, I will soon join you in the matrimonial estate. We must wait for her first mourning to be over, and we intend to marry as you have: quietly at home. In this case, her home. You, Elizabeth, and Georgiana are all invited. I am certain Mother will send formal invitations once a date has been set. Just know that one is coming. I have already written to my superiors, resigning my commission.

I remember conversations you and I have had about our futures. I have al-

ways been hesitant to allow myself to be leg-shackled to anyone, but I can say now with all sincerity that I find myself happy. Happier than I have been for a long time. I have always been fond of Anne, as you know. More than fond, even. To discover that her feelings have matched mine all these years brings a sense of joy that I never thought to experience.

I will stop now before one of us begins to weep. You can expect us all, including my betrothed, at your wedding on Friday. We look forward to supporting you on this most important day.

Yours,

RF

Darcy sat back with a smile on his face. "So, you proposed to Anne. I told you she liked you." He laughed and set the note aside, a grin on his face. Then, he spent the rest of the morning alternately attending to the remainder of his correspondence and thinking about Elizabeth.

~~~***~~~

Friday morning dawned clear and cold. Or, at least, Elizabeth assumed it did. The typical London haze of coal smoke blocked most of the sunlight. What it was not was rainy or snowing, and that was all she needed to feel as though the day was starting off well. A knock on her chamber door pulled her attention away from the window, and she called for the person to enter.

The door began to open and Jane stuck her head around it. "Are you up? Would you like some company?"

Elizabeth laughed. "I am up, as you well knew before you asked. Come in and sit with me. We have not had much of an opportunity in the last few days to talk." She moved to the bed and took her sister's hand when Jane joined her.

"I hesitated to bother you so early, despite your usual habits." Jane looked down at their joined hands. "I know you still suffer nightmares. If you were getting actual restful sleep, I did not want to wake you."

It was Elizabeth's turn to look down. She sighed, closing her eyes for a moment before looking up. "I do still have nightmares. I fear it will take time for them to subside." She smirked. "I feel badly for Mr. Darcy; if he chooses to share my bed every night, he will spend his days as tired as I do."

Jane giggled. "The poor man." She winked, making Elizabeth laugh, as well, but then grew serious again. "Are you happy, Lizzy? I know you entered into this engagement unwillingly, but you seem to have grown more content as the days have passed. Are you certain you still wish to marry him?"

"I am more certain than ever." Elizabeth whispered the words, her eyes filling with tears. "I love him, Jane, and he loves me. We shared our feelings with each other a few days ago ... the day ..." She trailed off, unable to speak of what had happened to her.

Jane understood exactly what her sister was trying to say. "This past Monday."

Elizabeth nodded and looked up from where her gaze had fallen. "So, I am no longer marrying a stranger. Instead, I am marrying a man I love, respect, and esteem, just as I always wanted to." She shook her head when she noticed tears in Jane's eyes. "Do not cry for me. I am happy. Very happy." She sighed and then grinned. "I did not know it was possible to be this happy, as a matter of fact."

Jane wiped her eyes with a square of linen she dug out of her sleeve. "I am so pleased. I have worried for you."

Elizabeth lifted her chin. "Well, do not. Mr. Darcy and I have determined that we will be the model of infatuation and love in our circle and that all of our acquaintance will want to know how we manage it." She laughed when her sister giggled again.

Jane threw her arms around Elizabeth. "I hope to one day have the same. I love you, Lizzy."

Elizabeth hugged her oldest sister and

dearest friend in return. "I love you, as well." She pulled back. "When your Mr. Bingley realizes his feelings for you, you will no doubt tell me you are happier than I could ever be, because you are far more good than I am."

Jane laughed, but a blush turned her cheeks pink. "He is not my Mr. Bingley." She lowered her head but looked up at her sister at the same time. "Not yet, anyway."

Elizabeth laughed. "Aunt told me that he has asked you for a courtship."

Lifting her head, Jane grinned. "She is correct. He spoke to Papa last night, after he asked me and I consented. He plans to get in touch with Uncle Philips about leasing Netherfield. My father told him it is free for at least the next quarter. If he lets it, we can see each other every day. Perhaps I will be in your shoes before summer."

"That would be wonderful! You must write to me and keep me apprised of your progress."

A knock on the door interrupted their chat. Annabelle walked in behind Elizabeth's newly-hired lady's maid, Jenny.

"Good morning, Lizzy. Good morning, Jane." She kissed the cheek of each niece, then straightened and clasped her hands. "Have you broken your fasts yet?" When she determined that they had not, she sent Jenny to the kitchen for a tray. Turning back to the girls, she spoke again. "It is almost time to dress for the wedding. Lizzy, your maid has asked for hot water for a bath, and the footmen should be bringing it up shortly. Jane, Mindy will assist you today. She has been training with my maid and can use the practice. She is a sweet girl and I think she will do well by you."

"I will be happy to assist in her training." Jane smiled. "How are Papa and Uncle this morning?"

"They seem to be well. I think your father is a bit melancholy, but I reminded him that, though he is losing his favorite out of his household, he still has you for a little while."

Jane blushed again. "He does." She sighed. "But hopefully not for long."

Elizabeth and Annabelle giggled, then laughed harder when Jane realized how bad her statement sounded and stumbled over her words trying to correct them.

"All is well, Jane." Elizabeth gasped the words as she tried to rein in her laughter. "I knew what you meant."

Jane rolled her eyes and shook her head, pressing her lips closed to keep them from twitching.

Eventually, the laughter subsided and the three chatted while the tray of breakfast foods, tea, and chocolate was delivered and they partook.

"Elizabeth, I hear the tub being filled. I want to share something with you to relieve a possible concern that I fear is hanging over you."

Elizabeth's brow creased. "What is it?"

"The magistrate visited yesterday while you were resting. He confirmed that his investigation results were accepted by the court and that no further action will be taken regarding that man." Annabelle reached over and took Elizabeth's hand as she spoke. "You can move on with your life knowing that what happened that day will never see the light or be spoken of again. You are free of that burden."

With a slow nod, Elizabeth took in her aunt's words. She swallowed. "That is good to hear." She paused. "I am relieved. I confess that in the back of my mind, I was concerned about it. It does not erase the memories, but ..." She straightened her spine and lifted her chin. "I will endeavor to do as I always do: look to the past only as it gives me pleasure."

"That is the spirit!" Annabelle smiled. "I caution you not to ignore the feelings, though. Feel them when they come. Cry if you must. Only then can you truly let them go."

"I will do that." Elizabeth threw her arms around her aunt's neck. "Thank you for all you have done. I love you."

"I love you, too, my dear girl." She squeezed her younger niece tightly for a long moment, then pulled away. "Come; let us get you married, shall we?"

~~~***~~~

Elizabeth's wedding to Darcy was everything she ever dreamed of. Held at Darcy House in the front parlor and presided over by Darcy's relative, the archbishop, it followed the same ceremonial pattern as all marriage ceremonies do.

Mrs. Bennet and the younger Bennet daughters had arrived in London the previous afternoon and had stayed, along with Mr. Bennet, with the Gardiners in Gracechurch Street. They were delivered to Darcy House shortly before the ceremony. Darcy had sent his coach to pick them and the Gardiners up and would have them taken home later in the afternoon.

While Mrs. Bennet was as excitable as ever, especially about meeting an earl and a countess, Darcy and his relations were able to tolerate her reasonably well, mostly by ignoring her.

When the wedding was over, the breakfast was eaten, and the guests farewelled, Darcy and his bride spent a pleasurable evening in the master's chambers talking, laughing, and doing what married couples all over the world do. Late that night, as they lay in each other's arms nearly asleep, he whispered one more thing to his new wife.

"I am so grateful that I found you. What started out as a mere honorable proposal turned into the best thing that ever happened to me. I love you."

With a sleepy smile, Elizabeth lifted her

head to accept her husband's kiss. "We are of one accord, for you are the best thing that ever happened to me, as well. I love you, too."

The End

Before you go ...

If you enjoyed this book, please consider leaving a review at the store where you purchased it.

Also, consider joining my mailing list at https://mailchi.mp/ee42ccbc6409/zoeburtonsignup

~Zoe

About the Author

Zoe Burton first fell in love with Jane Austen's books in 2010, after seeing the 2005 version of Pride and Prejudice on television. While making her purchases of Miss Austen's novels, she discovered Jane Austen Fan Fiction; soon after that she found websites full of JAFF. Her life has never been the same. She began writing her own stories when she ran out of new ones to read.

Zoe lives in a 100-plus-year-old house in the snow-belt of Ohio with her Boxer, Jasper. She is a former Special Education Teacher, and has a passion for romance in general, *Pride and Prejudice* in particular, and stock car racing.

Connect with Zoe Burton

Email:
zoe@zoeburton.com

Facebook Author page:
https://www.facebook.com/ZoeBurtonBooks

Burton's Babes Facebook Readers Group:
https://www.facebook.com/groups/BurtonsBabes/

Website:
https://zoeburton.com

Support me at Patreon:
https://www.patreon.com/zoeburtonauthor

Join my mailing list:
https://mailchi.mp/ee42ccbc6409/zoeburtonsignup

Pinterest:
https://www.pinterest.com/zoeburtonauthor/

More by Zoe Burton

Regency Single Titles:

I Promise To…

Lilacs & Lavender

Promises Kept

Bits of Ribbon and Lace

Decisions and Consequences

Mr. Darcy's Love

Darcy's Deal

The Essence of Love

Matches Made at Netherfield

Darcy's Perfect Present

Darcy's Surprise Betrothal

To Save Elizabeth

Darcy Overhears

Merry Christmas, Mr. Darcy!

Darcy's Secret Marriage

Darcy's Christmas Compromise

Darcy's Predicament

Darcy's Uneasy Betrothal

Darcy's Yuletide Wedding

Darcy's Unwanted Bride

Darcy's Favorite

Darcy's Christmas Scheme

Mr. Darcy: The Key to Her Heart

Darcy's Happy Compromise

Victorian Romance:

A MUCH Later Meeting

WESTERN ROMANCE:

Darcy's Bodie Mine

Bundles:

Darcy's Adventures

Forced to Wed

Promises

Mr. Darcy Finds Love (available exclusively to newsletter subscribers)

The Darcy Marriage Series Books 1-3

Mr. Darcy, My Hero

Coming Together

Christmas in Meryton

The Darcy Marriage Series:

Darcy's Wife Search

Lady Catherine Impedes

Caroline's Censure

Pride & Prejudice & Racecars

Darcy's Race to Love

Georgie's Redemption

Darcy's Caution